He stood in the cen
looking around like he'd never seen his
own house.

She followed Anson's gaze to the built-in shelves she'd filled with precious and painful memories. Things she wasn't ready to share with him. Before he could ask any questions, she opened the front door.

"Even though we were coerced, thank you for carrying her home. And for the house tour." Their "moment" in his bedroom flashed before her. *Damn, why'd I bring that up?*

"Anytime." Anson's blue-eyed gaze danced with amusement before he ducked his head and stepped outside. "Sleep well, Tess."

Fat chance of that.

She closed the door to prevent herself from watching him walk away. Tonight, Anson hadn't treated her indifferently like he had before and, in fact, he appeared to be fighting his own temptations. Part of the time, shutters seemed to fall over his eyes as he distanced himself, then she'd blink and he'd be wearing his devil's grin, drawing her in with flirtation. Maybe he wasn't as immune to their attraction as she'd thought.

"I can't figure you out, Chief Anson Curry. But why am I even bothering?"

* * *

HOME TO OAK HOLLOW:
New starts under the Texas sky

Dear Reader,

Welcome to the Texas Hill Country! Thank you for reading my debut Harlequin Special Edition novel, *A Sheriff's Star*, the first book in my Home to Oak Hollow series. I couldn't be more excited to share this story. My oldest son was the inspiration for this book. Being the mother of a child with Down syndrome has taught me to appreciate the little things and look at life in a new way.

A Sheriff's Star is about acceptance and having the courage to love again. Upon their arrival in the quaint Texas town, Tess Harper and her four-year-old daughter, Hannah, meet their landlord and neighbor, Chief Anson Curry—whom Hannah insists on calling Sheriff. He is the danger-seeking type Tess avoids, but her daughter adores him and his matchmaking grandmother, making it difficult for these two wounded hearts to avoid one another. Can a little girl with Down syndrome teach them that scars heal and love is worth the risk?

I hope you enjoy *A Sheriff's Star* and that you'll visit Oak Hollow again when the second and third books in the series are released. I love hearing from readers. You can find all of my social media at makennalee.com.

Happy reading!

Makenna Lee

A Sheriff's Star

MAKENNA LEE

HARLEQUIN
SPECIAL
EDITION

Recycling programs
for this product may
not exist in your area.

ISBN-13: 978-1-335-89492-2

A Sheriff's Star

Copyright © 2020 by Margaret Culver

Harlequin Enterprises ULC
22 Adelaide St. West, 40th Floor
Toronto, Ontario M5H 4E3, Canada
www.Harlequin.com

Printed in U.S.A.

Makenna Lee is an award-winning romance author living in the Texas Hill Country with her real-life hero and their two children. Her writing journey began when she mentioned all her story ideas and her husband asked why she wasn't writing them down. The next day she bought a laptop, started her first book and knew she'd found her passion. Makenna is often drinking coffee while writing, reading or plotting a new story. Her wish is to write books that touch your heart, making you feel, think and dream.

Books by Makenna Lee

Home to Oak Hollow

A Sheriff's Star

Visit the Author Profile page
at Harlequin.com for more titles.

To my sweet Lee Samuel.
Being your mother has made me a better human.
I love you with all of my heart!

Chapter One

Where's my baby?

Tess Harper's rib cage rattled with the abrupt drumming of her heart. "Hannah Lynn! Where are you? Answer Momma!"

This can't be happening! I only glanced away for a second.

Blood pounded in her head with such force her vision wavered, and a hot, prickly knot wedged in her throat. She grabbed a rack of clothes, knocked items to the floor and forced herself to focus. No one had been standing near them to snatch her little girl. Her precocious child must've slipped into one of the stuffed, round racks to play her favorite game of hide-and-seek.

Please, please let her be okay. "Hannah Lynn, answer me!"

A store employee stood nearby folding T-shirts, unaffected by Tess's cries.

"My daughter is missing! Can you make an announcement?"

"What does she look like?" asked the blank-faced teen.

"She's four, blonde, has Down syndrome."

"Over here, ma'am," a deep, male voice called from across the women's department. "I think I have who you're looking for."

Tess spun to see her daughter in the arms of a tall police officer. She ran, dodging obstacles and other shoppers, and pulled Hannah into her arms. The slight weight of her child was an immediate relief. She cradled her head of silky curls and kissed her smooth, broad forehead. "Don't you ever run off like that again. You scared the life out of me."

Hannah's bottom lip poked out and she placed both hands on her mother's cheeks. "I sorry, Momma."

The waning adrenaline rush left her trembling and dizzy. A strong arm wrapped around her shoulders and she stiffened. "I'm fine."

"Let's find a place to sit."

Allowing a strange man to touch her wasn't typical behavior, but he was a police officer like her father had been, and at the moment, she welcomed the support. "I could sit for a minute."

He guided them to a bench near the dressing

room and sat beside them. "Can I get you anything? Water?"

Tess shook her head, too intent on hugging her squirming daughter and savoring her baby shampoo scent. "I can't believe I let this happen. I only turned my head, and when I looked back, she was gone. What if…" Her throat tightened and burned with repressed tears, cutting off her words. Terrible scenarios scrolled through her mind, each one more horrifying than the next.

"Play hide-see, Momma."

"Sweet girl, you have to promise to tell me *before* we start playing hide-and-seek."

"Something like this happens to every parent at some point," said the officer. "Don't be too hard on yourself."

She cut him a hard look, ready to argue that her slipup was completely unacceptable. "Are you a parent?"

His jaw tightened and twitched. "No."

"Then you don't know what this feels like." Tess didn't miss the spark of sorrow in the man's blue eyes. His expression almost matched the strained one that often stared back from her reflection. She took a deep breath. "Thank you, though. Where did you find my daughter?"

"She found me. I was looking through the ladies' robes when a little hand reached out and tugged on my pant leg."

"Ladies' robes?" She bit her lip. It was none of her business what he shopped for.

Color bloomed high on his cheekbones. "For my grandmother."

Hannah wiggled off her mother's lap and onto the bench between them. "Sheriff safe?" Her blue-green eyes cut back and forth between them.

"Yes, baby." Tess glanced at his badge that read *Chief of Police*. "She thinks you're a sheriff like one of her favorite cartoon characters."

He smiled at Hannah, showing dimples almost hidden beneath a short-cropped, blond beard. "You sure are a smart little girl. How old are you?"

"I four." Hannah climbed onto her knees and traced around the border of his badge. "Circle." Her tiny finger poked through each of the holes surrounding the center star. "Sheriff star."

"It means I've promised to protect and keep you safe." He reached into his pocket, pulled out a small plastic star and pinned it onto Hannah's pink shirt. "You can be my honorary officer."

Her daughter—normally shy around men—flung her arms around his neck. "Tank you."

Tess once again caught a quick flash of distress before he schooled his features and returned the hug. Watching her child interact with a "father figure" set off a familiar swell of sadness that rolled in like a tidal wave. Hannah's father didn't want to be part of their lives, but he was the one missing out on the unconditional love of a precious child.

His loss. Idiot, selfish bastard.

She shook off the dark thoughts and took a good look at the man wearing a tan cowboy hat. His movie-star-worthy face topped powerful shoulders and a chest that filled his uniform shirt almost to the point of bursting buttons.

What's the matter with me? How can I notice a man's appearance at a time like this?

Eyes squeezed closed, she turned her head to hide her emotions from a man who was way too attractive, and no doubt knew it. He probably had women fawning all over him. She did not need another man who'd play with her heart like a chew toy. Especially one with a dangerous job.

I can, and will, raise my child on my own.

Oak Hollow, Texas, might be a small town, but she made up her mind to keep as much distance as possible between her and this tempting officer. It wouldn't be that hard. They'd only be here a couple of months before moving on to Houston to prepare for Hannah's heart surgery.

Hannah plopped onto her bottom, little legs swinging as she admired her prize.

"Thank you for your help. I need to find our shopping cart and get groceries. I'm moving into our new place today and I don't want to be late meeting the landlord."

He cocked his head and studied her with a set of stormy blue eyes. "Is your new place by any chance the Craftsman bungalow on Eighteenth Street?"

Hair lifted on the back of her neck. "How'd you know?"

He stuck out his hand. "Nice to meet you, Tess Harper. I'm your landlord, Anson Curry."

You've got to be kidding me.

Her mind spun for something to say. She took his offered hand, then jerked hers away as a powerful jolt zinged up her arm. "I didn't realize my new landlord was the town's chief of police."

The radio on his belt crackled and he adjusted the volume, then stood. "I wear a lot of different hats. Finish your shopping and meet me at the house whenever you're done. No rush."

"We won't be long."

"Bye-bye, sheriff."

He chuckled. "See you soon." With a wave, he turned to go, talking into his radio as he went.

Not daring to let go of her daughter's hand, she couldn't resist admiring his tall powerful frame as he moved through the store and out of sight. Her self-indulgent ogling caused a flash of embarrassment, and she glanced around, hoping no one had witnessed her moment of weakness.

"I have an idea. Let's be on the same team and play hide-and-seek with our shopping cart. Do you know where it is?"

"I find." Hannah tugged her mother's arm and set off on the search.

They found it quickly, but Tess was too frazzled to continue shopping. Residual panic still fluttered through her veins and getting out of public with her child clutched against her heart was all she could focus on.

Once they were safely enclosed in their SUV, she was able to breathe normally and pulled out of the retail store's parking lot. GPS directions led them from the modern outskirts of town to the historic district's tree-lined streets. An eclectic mix of well-kept homes from several different eras perched under the sweeping branches of oak trees. Manicured yards and Halloween decorations spoke of a community filled with pride and family values.

When Tess had seen the online photo of the moss green and rust-colored Craftsman home for rent, she couldn't resist a chance to live in the house for a couple of months. She just hadn't counted on the owner being more tempting than the historic property.

Just because Chief Curry is my landlord doesn't mean I'll have to see him very often.

Even though it was the middle of October, the day had been warm. Anson turned down the air conditioner in the old house he'd bought next door to the Curry ancestral home. But after his grandmother Nan's stroke, just being next door hadn't been enough for his peace of mind. Renting his home had been the best option.

He almost hadn't accepted Tess Harper's request for a month-to-month lease and for the home to remain furnished. The idea of strangers using his fur-

niture was disconcerting, but once he'd found out
she was in town to help the historical society open
the Oak Hollow history museum, his resistance wavered. He hoped getting his grandmother involved
in the museum would bring a spark back to her eyes
and encourage her to live again.

While he waited for his new tenants, he wandered
through the rooms he'd once shared with his wife.
The first bedroom was pale yellow and just right
for the little girl. Having a four-year-old next door
was going to be a painful reminder of the children
he'd planned to hear running across these creaky
wooden floors.

He scrubbed a hand over his face, trying to erase
the memory of his ex-wife telling him there was no
baby, begging and crying for him to forgive her cruel
deceptions. A familiar anger cramped his gut.

A knock on the door pulled him out of his miserable past. "Come in," he called out, and headed toward the front door.

Tess opened it a crack and peeked inside. "I guess
we have the right place?"

"Sure do. Come on in."

She stepped inside, gasped and turned in a circle.
"This is fabulous. Other than opening up the wall
between the kitchen and living room, most of the
original Craftsman architecture is still intact."

Hannah darted past her mother and spun around
the living room like a mini ballerina. "Where my
room?"

"Hannah Lynn, be polite and say hello to Chief Curry."

The little girl hugged his knees. "Hi."

Paternal pangs stirred in his chest. "Hello, Hannah. Go look in that first room and see if you like it."

On the toes of her little red patent leather shoes, she walked down the hall to explore.

Tess kneeled in front of the fireplace and rubbed her fingers across the green tile around the firebox. "I'd bet anything this is the original Batchelder tile. You've kept it in great condition."

"I've only owned it for four years. Before that it was the Walton family home. Follow me, and I'll show you the rest of the house."

Her eyes narrowed as she stood and glanced from him to the door. "No need. I'm sure you're busy and have things to do."

He'd grown used to the single women of Oak Hollow plying him with baked goods and promises of home-cooked meals. Fluttering their lashes and trying to get him into bed or down the aisle. Flirting to the point that his dispatcher, Betty, teased him about what she called the "Pantie Posse."

Not this woman. She wanted him gone. Not in her bed.

"I'll get out of your way. Keys are on the counter with a copy of the lease."

"It's the month-to-month lease we talked about over emails?"

"Yes. Are you sure you don't want to switch to a six month? It's cheaper."

Long waves of mahogany-brown hair swung around her shoulders. "Can't do that. It should take about two months to complete my job here and then we have to move to Houston."

"For your next job?"

"For Hannah's…" Her voice cracked and she caught her trembling lip with her teeth, then glanced down the short hallway where her daughter sang at full volume. "Yes."

What did she stop herself from saying? "Let me know if you have any questions about the house or the town."

"I'll call if I do."

"If my truck is in the driveway, you can always knock on my door."

She spun to face him. "What door? Where do you live?"

He hitched a thumb over his shoulder. "Next door in the big white house."

Her green eyes widened. "In the fabulous Victorian with the wraparound porch?"

"That's the one. It's been in the Curry family since it was built."

Hannah ran in and pulled on her mother's shirt. "I hungry, Momma."

"I'll make you a peanut butter sandwich."

"Nooo," Hannah wailed, and tossed her head back. "Mac a chee."

She picked up her fussy child. "We don't have any mac and cheese."

"No sandwich." The toddler buried her face against her mother's neck.

Embarrassment and exhaustion were clear on Tess's pretty, heart-shaped face. The sudden urge to tuck a lock of hair behind her ear and pull them both into his arms surprised him. Instead, he hooked his thumbs in his pockets and stepped farther away.

"After losing her in Target, I just had to get out of there. I didn't get groceries."

The little girl kicked her legs. "No sandwich."

Tess struggled to hold on to her when she arched her back. "Hannah Lynn Harper, this is not the way to behave if you want to be Chief Curry's honorary officer."

Hannah's head popped up and her little mouth formed an O. "I be good."

Anson pressed his lips together to hide the smile and glanced at his watch. "I need to run and pick up dinner for my grandmother, Nan, and The Acorn Cafe has the best macaroni and cheese. Can I bring an order?"

Hannah bounced in her mother's arms. "Mac a chee, pease."

Tess adjusted her child on her hip and shot him a narrow-eyed glance.

Before she could speak, he held up a hand. "It's no trouble. Consider it a welcome to town meal. What would you like?"

"Nothing for me, thanks." She set Hannah on her feet.

"Momma, packpack, pease."

"Your backpack is in the car." Keys jingled as she pulled them from her pocket. "I'll get it, but you have to take a bath before Chief Curry gets back with your food."

He winked at Hannah. Her giggle made him smile, but also struck a wounded place inside him. A place that longed for a little one of his own. He held the front door open and motioned for Tess to go out ahead of him.

After a moment of hesitation, she quickly stepped past him, keeping as much distance between them as possible.

This woman doesn't even want to be near me.

She rushed ahead and unlocked a maroon SUV with an attached rental trailer.

"You'll need help unloading," he said.

"I'll be fine. I got it packed into the trailer all by myself, and I can get it out." She swung a pink sparkly backpack over one shoulder, retrieved a large suitcase with one hand and tried to grab a box off the floorboard with the other.

He rushed forward and lifted the box. "I've got it."

"Please be careful with it." Her tone altered from all business to concern.

Anson glanced at the neatly printed writing. *Dad and Shawn's flags and photos.* Was Shawn her husband? Were they flags that had draped coffins?

When she had the front door open, she put down the suitcase, then turned and took the box from him. "Thanks." She clutched it to her chest, gazed down at the names across the top, then turned away like she'd forgotten he was there.

"I'll be back in about thirty minutes," he called after her and closed the door.

Anson drove the three blocks to Oak Hollow town square and went inside The Acorn Cafe. "Hey, Sam," he said to the owner. "How's the family?"

"All good." Sam glanced across the café and smiled at his wife, Dawn.

The love bouncing between the couple made Anson's chest tighten. They had what he longed for. A real connection, not a temporary hook-up.

It took several minutes to greet various people before taking a seat on a stool at the old-fashioned soda counter. One of the new waitresses sidled up so close her breasts brushed his arm.

"Evening, Anson," she crooned. "What's your pleasure tonight?"

He shifted out of her reach. "Hi, Tina. I need to place a to-go order."

"I'll be more than happy to get you anything you want."

Her emphasis of the word *anything* was not subtle, but he ignored the suggestive comment. "I need an order of mac and cheese with a side of fresh fruit and three orders of pot roast with mashed potatoes and green beans."

"You and your grandmother have company to-night?"

"New neighbors."

Once Tina wrote up the order and walked away, he called the station. "Hey, Walker. Need me to stop by before I go home for the night?"

"All quiet this evening, Chief. You work too many hours. You should call up one of those single ladies for a change."

"Think I'll leave that to you for now. See you to-morrow."

The kitchen door swung open, giving him an eye-ful of Tina undoing her top button and adjusting her breasts to swell even farther out the top of her uni-form. He rubbed his eyes and sighed. None of the ladies who chased him piqued his interest. Not like the attraction that had slapped him when he met his prickly new neighbor with the rigid, full mouth he'd like to soften under his kiss.

Just my luck the first woman I've wanted in ages is repelled by me.

Chapter Two

Hannah Lynn stood with her arms crossed and shook her head, making long curls swing across her face. "No, no, no!"

Tess closed her eyes, searching for patience. The seemingly unimportant lack of a bath mat had thrown their evening routine into a tailspin, but she'd forgotten having the right bath mat was her daughter's newest obsessive-compulsive trigger. "Hannah, they're packed in the boxes in the front of the moving trailer. I can't get to them tonight. Please, get into the water before it gets cold."

"Can't, Momma."

Tess grabbed the towel she'd planned to use,

folded it into the correct shape and placed it on the pale green mosaic tile floor.

Hannah eyed the makeshift mat, bent over to straighten one folded up corner, then finally climbed into the tub.

With that battle won, Tess grabbed the soap and sang the bath time song. "Bath time for my girl, bath time for my girl, bath time for my little bitty girl. Yee-haw." After a quick washing, she dried her wiggly daughter.

"My sheriff back?"

"Not yet. His name is Chief Curry."

"Chief, chief, chief." Hannah tried out the name in a singsong voice.

Exhaustion pushed at Tess, but she had to keep going and get them settled in before she gave in to sleep. "Please stand still and put your leg in your pajama pants."

Once she was dressed, the little girl ran down the short hallway, jumped onto the living room couch, and pulled dolls and books from her sparkly princess backpack. A knock at the door had her springing back to her feet.

"Hannah Lynn, do not open that door when you don't know who's on the other side." She stopped her precocious child just in time and looked out the peephole. There stood a wall of muscle and temptation, just waiting to throw a twist into her perfectly laid plan to do the job she'd been hired for, then move on. Her sudden urge to brush her hair and put on makeup irritated her further.

I can't be attracted to a man with a dangerous job. I won't risk the pain my mother and I suffered, twice.

She steadied her breath and turned the knob.

"My chief," Hannah cheered. "I hungry."

He chuckled and held out a plastic bag. "Here you go, little one."

"Tank you." Hannah rushed to the table in the breakfast nook off the living room.

Tess shook her head. "I was trying to teach her to say Chief Curry so she won't keep calling you sheriff."

"She can call me whatever she wants. Anything else I can do for you before I go?"

"Toys, pease," Hannah said as she took items out of the bag.

Tess crossed to the table and opened the container of mac and cheese. "They're in the U-Haul, sweetie. We'll get your boxes of toys in the morning." She held a foam box out to Anson. "This must be yours."

"I went ahead and got something for you, too."

"For me?" She opened the container of pot roast with mashed potatoes and green beans. Her annoyance with his presence faded slightly. "Thank you. How'd you know my favorite comfort food?" The broad smile and laugh lines around his eyes heightened his already devastating appearance, and she forced herself to look away. Experience had taught her it was highly doubtful his true character and moral fiber matched up to his shiny exterior. Her ex-husband had put on a good face at the beginning, but it had rapidly tarnished after saying I do.

"Lucky guess. I can bring in her toys."

"Yes, yes, yes," Hannah cheered.

Having this man around stole focus from her daughter, but she worked to keep the frustration from her expression. "I don't want to keep you from your dinner. You've done enough."

"Won't hurt me to bring in a few boxes."

A moan of delight came from Hannah as she took another big bite.

"I can't leave her to eat alone. She sometimes eats too fast and chokes."

"You stay with her. I'll get them."

This man is relentless. Still, she softened to him a smidgen more and held her keys out by the one that would open the trailer, admitting he was kind and helpful. But still off-limits.

He set a second bag on the table and took the keys. "I better leave my food inside. If I put it on the porch the neighbor's dog will eat it."

His nearness brought the scent of something woodsy and made her breath hitch. A flutter erupted to swirl in her belly, and she focused on her food in an effort not to watch him walk away. Her ex, Brent, never would've been thoughtful enough to see through her claim that she wasn't hungry, or looked so delicious in a pair of uniform pants.

I'd like to see the chief in a pair of faded jeans

and... She bit her bottom lip. Hard. *Shut up, disobedient brain.*

"Momma, eat."

She sat beside Hannah, grabbed a plastic fork and savored a bite of tender beef dripping with gravy. "This is so good. Slow down, sweetie, and eat some of the fruit, too."

A few minutes later the door opened and Anson stepped inside carrying a stack of boxes. "Which bedroom?"

"The first one, please." She stayed seated beside her daughter and watched him haul his load down the hallway like it was nothing more than a pillow.

He walked back through the living room to the door.

"Wait. Don't forget your food."

"I'm going to get a few more boxes first. You have them well labeled and I saw some you might need before tomorrow."

Three times he came and went, carrying a stack much bigger than she could've managed.

"I locked the trailer." He hung the keys on a hook high on the doorframe.

Her ex-husband would've flicked his hand at someone else and told them to do all the work. "I appreciate your help, and the food. I was hungrier than I realized."

"Thought you might be." He picked up his bag and glanced at his watch. "I should get home before

Jenny leaves. She stays with my grandmother during the day."

"She lives with you next door?"

He adjusted his cowboy hat. "I moved in with Nan after she had a mild stroke. That's when I decided to put my house up for rent."

"I'm sorry to hear she's been ill. It's just the two of you in that big house?" Tess flinched, not even wanting to admit to herself that she was fishing to see if he was single.

"Yep. Lots of empty rooms."

"How's your grandmother recovering?"

"Better now, but..." He shrugged and pinched the bridge of his nose.

Why am I invading his private life and encouraging conversation? "I didn't mean to pry."

"It's okay. Nan has always been such a strong woman. A fighter. But she seems to be giving up this time." Light reflected off the face of his watch as he waved a hand like he could erase his words. "Didn't mean to dump all that on you. I'm just worried."

"I did ask. Sorry to hear she's struggling." Tears pricked the back of her eyes. "I went through something similar with my mom after—"

"Momma! I done." Hannah tapped her spoon on the table, then tilted her head back. "Sleepy."

Tess shoved aside painful memories of her mom's unnecessary death. "Okay, sweetie. We have to brush your teeth before you fall asleep."

"No, no, no." Her repeated gesture looked as if she was conducting a symphony. "No teeth."

"You won't have any teeth if we don't brush them." She got no response and glanced at Anson. "The word 'no' is her current favorite."

He did a poor job of hiding his grin. "I'll get out of your way and let you get her to bed. You ladies have a nice evening."

Tess followed him to the door. Before she thought better of it, she put a hand on his forearm, but quickly slid her fingers away. His shifting eyes and change in breathing told her he'd definitely noticed the primal flash. "I'm sorry we used so much of your time this evening. I promise things aren't usually this crazy. I've never lost her before. Again, thanks for everything, Chief Curry."

One brow rose along with one corner of his full mouth. "Call me Anson. We're neighbors after all."

"Okay." But she couldn't make herself say his name.

"Should I call you Mrs. Harper or Hannah's Momma?"

"It's Ms. Harper, but I think Tess is the best option."

He touched the brim of his cowboy hat with two fingers. "Good night, Tess."

"Good night… Anson." She locked the door and rested her forehead against the polished wood. He was a temptation she couldn't afford to indulge, but boy, was he one hard-to-resist man.

Hannah wrapped her arms around her mother's legs. "I want Boo Bunny."

Her baby girl's hair was silky soft under her fingers and she couldn't resist pulling her up into her arms. "You're right. It will feel more like home if your animal friends are in your room. You can unpack them while I put sheets on the beds."

Tess got to work while Hannah arranged her animals in a very particular order. Once the battle of the teeth brushing was won, she settled her sleepy-eyed child under the covers and they read *Barnyard Dance* and *Goodnight Moon*. She gave her a dose of liquid Lasix to help with fluid retention, then tucked her in with the usual routine of a kiss on each cheek, her nose and forehead.

"Good night, sweetie. Momma loves you."

"Wuv you, Momma."

The faint illumination of the last remnants of daylight faded from the window. Moments later, her precious child drifted into dreams. They were all each other had. It had been that way since she went to the hospital alone. Gave birth alone. Then brought her new, fragile baby daughter home to a tiny apartment.

Alone.

"Sweet dreams, my beautiful girl. I pray I can give you a long, happy, fulfilled life."

Tess blew a kiss, got toiletries from her suitcase, then ran a bubble bath. With her long hair twisted up in a clip, she eased into the hot water, but her mind wouldn't settle. Something about this move to a small, family-oriented town was pulling up painful memories of the day her ten-month marriage abruptly ended. Stripping her of the new family that was supposed to embrace her and make her feel part of something again.

She closed her eyes, and as much as she resisted, her mind replayed the evening a phone call changed her world...

"Good evening, Tess," said her doctor. "I have the results from your amniocentesis. They tell us your baby girl has Down syndrome."

It was the last thing she heard. She couldn't remember saying goodbye or hanging up the phone. Shock left her mute and crumpled on the floor against the kitchen cabinets.

But I'm twenty-seven. Doesn't this only happen to older mothers? She'd been sure the blood test had been a false positive, but it hadn't.

Brent walked in, trailed by his overbearing mother. "What are you doing on the floor? Who was on the phone?" he asked. But even with his child growing inside her, he didn't bend down to see if she was okay or pick her up.

"Doctor. Our baby..." Tess cradled her expanding belly and rocked. "Our baby has Down syndrome."

He stared at her, sat in the closest chair and didn't utter a sound.

As usual, his mother had no trouble expressing

her thoughts. "Well, that's unfortunate. But we can get this taken care of."

She clutched tighter to the swell of her unborn daughter. "It's not something you can take care of with medicine or surgery. No doctor can change it."

Her mother-in-law rolled her eyes. "I know that. You can end this pregnancy, then try again."

The matter-of-fact tone sliced like a blade.

"End it?" Tess blinked back tears. "I would never..." Each breath was a fight against the cloying pressure squeezing her chest. A new version of panic pushed at her mind, pushed at her heart, making each beat a hammer strike. "Brent, say something. Tell her we'd never do that."

He stared at her, then glanced at his mother like a little boy begging for mommy to fix his problems.

Her look of authority bored into her son. "Brent, you know what has to be done."

For a desperate second, Tess almost believed he'd do the right thing this time. He'd stand up to his mother. Just this once. He had to.

She was wrong, of course.

Tess splashed her bathwater, bringing herself back into the present. Bubbles slid down her cheeks as she worked to ease her ragged breath.

Marrying the son of a bitch had been her first stupid move, but she'd fallen for Brent Wilcott hard and fast. During the months they'd dated in grad school, he'd appeared confident and full of charm. When he'd gone on and on about how his family would love her and take her in as one of their own, it had been like icing on the cake. She'd longed to feel like part of a family again. *Needed* it. But the things Brent told her couldn't have been further from the truth.

Once they married and moved into the family home, she got her first real glimpse of Brent's true personality. And the family that had seemed so up-standing, so loving, wasn't at all what she'd expected. Ever so slowly, she began to realize she'd mistaken control for affection. Brent's parents cared more about status than anything else, and her wimpy pushover of a husband had let them tell him what to do and think.

Using their connections, they streamlined arrangements for divorce papers and a large check. Days later, they had thrust both into her hands. The coldhearted treatment shouldn't have been a surprise, but had slapped her with bewilderment. They'd shut her and her unborn child out of their lives like an offensive book they'd just slammed closed. She hadn't wanted a dime of their money but took it for the sake of her special needs child.

Brent's abandonment had crushed the last part of her heart that was open to the possibility of loving another man. She wouldn't make that mistake again. Once was more than enough. There was only room for Hannah now. Her baby's love filled her up, and it was just the two of them against the world, while the

Wilcott family lived the high life in a Beacon Hill mansion, pretending they were perfect.

Her bathwater had grown cold so she dried off and dressed in an old nightshirt. She looked in on Hannah one more time but couldn't bring herself to get into her own bed. Maybe sleep would come after looking through the thick folder of information about the archivist job that had brought them to this charming town.

She spread photos of antiques and memorabilia across the coffee table, then turned on the stereo system Anson had left in the living room. A forgotten CD started to play. A lone guitar strummed a slow melody accompanied by a soulful male voice. The lilting tune filled the room with soothing, bluesy crooning. Something about the deep voice and sad song made her think of Anson.

What would it be like to dance with him? Would he hold her close against his broad chest, cradling her in his strong arms?

The song changed, but she was still standing in front of the speakers, swaying to the music. Concentrating on work wasn't going to happen tonight. Tomorrow, after she saw the space she'd be working with, would be soon enough.

But there was one more task she wanted accomplished before getting into bed. She unpacked the two triangle box frames holding flags from her father's and brother's funerals. The built-in shelves on each side of the fireplace were the perfect place to display them. Her father's military and police officer photos flanked his flag. A family portrait of the four of them took its place in the center next to one of her mother. Her older brother's Navy picture and flag sat to the right. A smiling, childhood shot of the two of them at the beach in San Diego finished the display.

With that completed, she decided to unpack one box of kitchen items, then go to bed. She'd be more than grateful for the coffeepot in the morning.

Anson stood in the door of his grandmother's antique-filled bedroom. "Nan, do you need anything else before I go to bed?" The smile he'd known his whole life wasn't in place.

"No, dear. I'm fine." She smoothed the comforter with arthritic fingers that used to create magic in the gardens—before she'd given up on living.

He tried one more idea. "Want to get out of the house and visit with some of the ladies tomorrow? I could drive you over to Mary's for coffee."

"Not tomorrow. You go get some sleep. I'm just going to finish watching this old episode of *Murder She Wrote*."

"Okay. Good night." He stopped in the kitchen, prepped the coffee for morning and grabbed the last chocolate cookie. After locking the front door, he took a shower and fell into bed.

The branch of an oak tree tap-tapped against his bedroom window, throwing shadows that danced across the ceiling. Normally, he fell asleep quickly, but every time he closed his eyes, the dark-haired temptress next door invaded his mind. With expressive emerald eyes above her wide, full mouth, she had an appeal that had grabbed him and refused to let go.

He was known for his ability to read people, and his intriguing new neighbor had her guard zipped up tighter than a sealed juvenile file. Not to mention the sad defensiveness clouding her eyes. He'd bet money it had something to do with Hannah's missing and unmentioned father.

That kind of feeling was familiar. He'd married his ex-wife after she claimed to be pregnant. But the marriage had been filled with empty promises and deceit.

Since his divorce, he'd had countless opportunities to date, or hook up for the night, but none of the women had interested him enough to brave the dangers of dating under the watchful eyes of Oak Hollow. His love life—or lack thereof—was already like the movie of the week. Dating a local woman would be opening up a can of disaster that would shake up his simple world.

He threw off the covers and went out onto the back porch. A cool October breeze blew, but the canvas cushions on the porch swing were still warm from the heat of the day and felt soothing against his bare back.

The stray tomcat who'd adopted Nan's backyard jumped up onto the porch.

"What's up, Tom-Tom. No cage fights or ladies to visit tonight?"

The beat-up, old gray-and-white cat tried to meow, but it came out a broken croaking sound. Years of catfights had left him with an injured voice box and scars on his permanently bent ear. Tom-Tom hopped onto the far corner of the porch swing, spun around once and settled down to groom himself, all the while keeping a watchful eye. Anson had yet to touch the skittish animal and this was the first time he'd dared to sit this close.

"Finally getting used to me? Guess it's just us two lonely bachelors." *Lonely? Am I lonely?* Anson sighed, rubbed his eyes and admitted he was, in fact, lonesome.

The kitchen light turned on in his old house next door. Was Tess restless tonight, too? Had she been in bed, warm and soft and sexy, only to get up when sleep wouldn't come?

The woman on his mind appeared at the double glass doors of the breakfast nook like a temptation ready to rock his world. Chills erupted across his skin. Her pink T-shirt hung off one shoulder and showed off long, toned legs, sculpted like an athlete's or dancer's. She raised her arms above her head and stretched, making her shirt ride higher and revealing a pair of black panties that made his breath snag.

Tess began to sway, dancing to music he couldn't hear, but her sensual movements created a melody his body heard loud and clear.

She opened the cardboard box on the table and pulled out dishes, all the while continuing to move in a slow, rhythmic dance. She twirled to the cabinets on the far wall, straightened one leg behind her, toes pointed as she reached to put a bowl on a top shelf. In a graceful pivot on one foot, she spun across the floor. Her long hair tumbled free from its clip and cascaded down her back.

He sat forward on the swing, wishing he was close enough to discover the texture of her hair. And feel those long legs wrapped around his hips. Anson swallowed hard and left his spot on the swing to stand at the edge of the porch, drawn by her graceful dance like stars to the night. It suddenly occurred to him that he was hidden in the dark watching without her knowledge. But he didn't turn away. Couldn't make himself.

I shouldn't have taken down the old curtains before I bought new ones. But I'm glad I did.

She broke down and folded the empty box, disappeared from view and the lights turned off. He continued to stare at the dark house. A house he'd planned to turn into a family home, raising a loud, happy family within its walls. His ex's deceptions had crushed that dream. Why was he wasting time thinking about a woman who showed no signs of wanting him? Especially since he couldn't—wouldn't—get involved with a woman who was leaving. The last thing he was looking for was another temporary relationship.

If there's a next time, it has to be the real thing. The forever thing.

The cat hopped up onto the railing beside him. He reached out slowly to scratch his head, but Tom-Tom hissed and scrambled away.

"Guess you need more time, old fella. I know the feeling. And I sense our pretty new neighbor feels the same." He glanced back at the darkened house. Why was this standoffish woman the first one he actually wanted in his bed in a long time? Was the blinding attraction the thrill of the unknown, or because Tess and Hannah represented the family that should've been? In the very house he'd expected to fill with children of his own.

"Think there are a few broken wings around here. Aren't we a pitiful trio," he said to the wary animal. Anson made up his mind to ignore the unexpected feelings she'd set off. No reason to start something that had no future.

He'd be a friendly neighbor but keep his distance from Tess Harper.

And buy her some window coverings.

Chapter Three

Tess woke to the sound of Hannah's wheezing breath coming through the baby monitor. She sat up and struggled with a moment of disorientation.

Where am I?

Her surroundings came into focus. New house. New town. The beginning of their new chapter. She swung her legs off the mattress and opened her suitcase. After pulling out the nebulizer and medication, she readied it for a breathing treatment. With practiced ease, she slipped the elastic strap around her daughter's small head and put the mask in place over her mouth and nose. A few minutes later her baby breathed normally. Tess settled beside her, one hand over Hannah's heart to assure her it still beat, but it was not beating as it should. She prayed nightly that her upcoming surgery would fix it.

It was six in the morning and sleep wouldn't return. Tess shuffled to the kitchen, grateful she'd unpacked the coffeepot before bed. Anson deserved another thank-you for carrying in the boxes without even being asked. Again, she couldn't help comparing him to her useless ex-husband.

While inhaling the nutty aroma of brewing coffee, she inspected the authenticity of the Shaker cabinets and brass hardware. The cherrywood gleamed with rich red tones and was buffed smooth from years of use. Old homes held secrets that begged for discovery, like the Celtic heart carved inside one panel. The butcher-block island felt wavy and softly pitted under her palm, and she imagined the many family meals prepared on its surface.

"What stories do you have to tell me? Any insight into the man who last lived here?"

Someday she'd fulfill her dream of owning a historic home, filled with the antiques she loved researching, but she couldn't spend that much of the huge settlement from the quickie divorce Brent's connections had secured. Not yet. Until Hannah's surgery bill was paid, the funds—tainted by the mandate to disappear from their lives—had to be conserved. The Wilcotts only wanted perfect people in their family. Rejection prodded the festering wound inside her.

The coffeepot chimed its success, and with hot caffeine in hand, she stepped out onto the small side porch off the kitchen. The sun glittered over the horizon, and the first golden rays glowed like a line of fire around the peaks of Anson's three-story house. A brisk breeze blew under her nightshirt, making her aware she wasn't dressed for public display. A greenbelt stretched behind them, so her hot landlord and his grandmother were the only ones with a view of her porch.

The hot landlord who's strictly off-limits.

And she was the only one that could see their much larger backyard, filled with overgrown flower beds and what looked to be an abandoned vegetable garden. His grandmother's poor health must be the reason for its neglected demise. But even in its current state, it held a unique beauty she wanted to capture in a watercolor painting.

Sun glinted off the glass roof of a Victorian greenhouse and she caught her breath. The old glass-and-metal structure was tucked in the back corner beside a huge magnolia tree. The best kind for climbing. Had Anson scaled its branches once upon a time? She imagined the yard in spring, overflowing with color and the sweet scents of honeysuckle and antique roses, and a young boy playing barefoot under the tree.

I'd like a yard like that where Hannah can run and play. After her surgery we can buy a home of our own.

Tess's doorbell chimed at seven forty-five that morning. The peephole revealed a stocky, dark-haired police officer. Her heart sprang into her throat and a painful childhood memory flashed. Her father's partner at the San Diego police department standing in their living room. Her mother breaking down into a heap on the floor. Daddy was never coming home.

Her mind raced with reasons an officer would be here this morning. *I have no one to fear dead. It's okay.* She pushed away her anxiety and opened the door. "Good morning. Can I help you?" She hoped he couldn't hear the tremble in her voice.

"Morning, ma'am. I'm Officer Luke Walker. Heard a rumor you have some boxes that need moving."

"Oh… Wow. Thank you." Before she could say more, she caught sight of Anson crossing into her yard. Her belly jumped with a mixture of desire and trepidation. His confident stride caused her pulse to race for an entirely different reason than the fear she'd felt only a moment ago. No doubt her new neighbor was responsible for the additional help.

He's really messing with my plan to keep my distance.

Hannah ran past her, stopped in front of Anson and twirled in her iridescent fairy costume. "My chief."

The easy smile reached his eyes. "Good morning, little one. Are you a princess today?"

"Fairy." She held out the purple-and-green skirt and twirled again. "And Momma."

"We have matching Halloween costumes," Tess

clarified, then grabbed the key from the hook by the door and stepped outside. "I didn't expect this kind of welcome, but I appreciate the help. I get the feeling this town is a place where everybody knows what everyone else is doing?"

Officer Walker laughed, his obsidian eyes twinkling with humor. "There's truth to that."

"Just helping out a neighbor," Anson said.

He didn't make eye contact or smile the way he had the evening before. He'd smiled at Hannah, but not at her. She ground her teeth, wanting to kick herself for caring, or even noticing. It was better this way. It's what she wanted.

Then why did it cause a hollowness in the pit of her stomach?

She walked past both men and opened the lock, then stood in the trailer to hand out boxes and her grandmother's rocking chair. When her fingers brushed Anson's, he jerked and backed away so quickly he almost dropped a box. After that, he talked casually with Walker, but kept his distance from her.

Maybe the sparks she'd felt the night before were only in her imagination. Maybe what she'd perceived as flirting was only a public servant welcoming someone to town. This was good. She'd already told herself anything with him would be a mistake.

Hannah cheered them along and danced through the yard while they worked. When everything had been unloaded, Tess stepped out of the trailer and adjusted her ponytail. An old lady stood at one of the side windows of Anson's house. Tess waved, but the woman wasn't looking at her. All of her attention was focused on the dancing child, a smile deepening the creases on her face.

Anson followed her gaze. "That's my grandmother, Nan." His head tilted. "I haven't seen her smile like that in a while. Not since my grandfather died."

"My sweet girl has that effect on people."

"She sure does."

Walker interrupted their observation. "I'm heading to the station."

"Wait," she said. "Can I get you a drink or something before you go?"

"No, thanks. I have coffee in my truck."

"I really appreciate your help this morning."

"Glad to be of service to our newest resident. See you at the station, Chief."

"I'll be right behind you." Anson waved as his officer got into a silver truck.

"Before you go, which way to the town square?" Tess said. "The GPS directions didn't take us that way when we drove in yesterday."

Anson motioned with his hand. "Three blocks that way and you'll come to the square."

"Which building is the museum? I'm supposed to meet Mrs. Grant there at two o'clock."

"It's the two-story red brick on the corner near the gazebo. You'll like Mary Grant."

"She seemed really nice on the phone." An awkward pause swirled between them.

"I should get to work. See you later." Without a backward glance, Anson crossed to his house, waving to Hannah on his way.

After convincing Hannah that her Halloween costume couldn't be worn to the grocery store, she and her daughter had a successful shopping trip, with no one getting lost. The star-shaped badge Anson had given Hannah was pinned proudly over her heart. It was her newest security item and worn at all times. Tess made a note to ask him for a backup badge as preemptive planning to prevent a possible meltdown.

Because she needed Hannah on her best behavior while meeting with the president of the historical society, Tess had taken extra care while preparing snacks. She put finger foods into individual baggies, just the way her daughter liked them. There were carrots chopped into circles, not sticks, Cheerios and super thin apple rings. Luckily, ovals were forgiven if the apple's shape didn't cooperate. Fingers crossed, the new favorite shape didn't make its way into snack time. Cutting food into stars would take forever.

Thank you so much, obsessive-compulsive disorder.

"Hannah Lynn, do you still have your boots on?"

"Yes, Momma." She danced into the kitchen and pointed to her chest. "And star."

The pure delight on her daughter's face was contagious, and some of the heaviness lifted from her chest. This precious child was the love of her life. "Good girl. Let's grab our jackets and your backpack of toys."

Since it was only three blocks to the town square, they decided to walk. Thank goodness they'd left home with extra time because Hannah was curious about everything they passed. Patterns in the brick sections of sidewalks, fading fall flowers sticking through white picket fences and every animal within a mile radius, all of them deemed "cute" by her loving daughter.

"I need you to be a very good girl today. Momma is meeting with an important lady."

"I be good. Look! Circle." Hannah did her awkward version of skipping, then studied the design on someone's mailbox, but shook her head. "Not it."

Tess hadn't yet figured out what magical circle her child sought, but apparently this one missed the mark. They walked around the corner of a two-story house and the town square came into view. A thrill zinged through Tess's history-loving soul. It sounded like a cliché, but the scene before them was a Norman Rockwell painting come to life. Not many towns had preserved their heritage as well as Oak Hollow.

The concrete sidewalks changed to red brick along the busy storefronts. Halloween decorations swayed in the light breeze and adorned the window displays, but Tess's attention was focused on the architecture of the structures rather than the items for sale. The center of the square was filled with mature oaks surrounding a white limestone courthouse, picnic area and a playground.

Hannah is going to notice it in three, two...

"Look, Momma! Swing."

"How exciting. We have to go to my new job, but we can stop and play for a few minutes."

"Minutes?" Sun glinted off the top of her head, highlighting the many colors in her wavy hair.

"I'll set the timer on my watch for ten minutes. When it chimes, I need you to be a big girl and help me find my new workplace."

"I be big girl."

After a short playground session, they located the correct building and walked into the spacious, 1900s red brick structure. Narrow plank Douglas fir floors spanned the whole length of the space. Exquisite woodwork surrounded every door and window. She stood in the center of the large empty room and gazed up at the pressed tin ceiling.

"You must be Tess and Hannah."

Tess spun around. "Yes, ma'am."

"We're so happy you're here to help us set up our museum."

She took the elegant, older woman's manicured hand. "It's a pleasure to meet you. I'm excited to get started. Hannah, say hello to Mrs. Grant."

"Please, call me Mary." She leaned down and held out her hand to Hannah. "Nice to meet you, young lady."

"Hi." Hannah gave her a sideways high five, bounced on her toes, then spun away to explore.

Mary chuckled and tucked a strand of her sleekly bobbed, silver hair behind her ear. "How old is she?"

"She's four. I promise she won't keep me from my work."

"If you do find that you need help, there are lots of wonderful people in Oak Hollow that would be more than happy to lend a hand. Myself included."

"I appreciate the offer. I want to make sure I understand all the aspects of this job. I'll authenticate, appraise value for insurance, interview and collect local history and stories to go with the items, and make sure they're displayed properly."

"That's perfect. More than we thought we could get from only one person." Mary smiled as they paused to watch Hannah.

She walked back and forth across the old wooden floor, singing a Disney song, and purposely stepping on each crack rather than avoiding them.

"My goal is to offer a full-service business that hits on all aspects of archiving and historical preservation. Any tips on where I should start with the local stories?"

"Yes. You'll want to talk to Cornelia Curry. She's one of our oldest residents and knows all the best stories about Oak Hollow. Several of the antiques for the museum are in her house."

"Curry? Chief Curry's grandmother?"

"Yes. You'll need to spend quite a bit of time with her."

Of course I will. Why is the universe determined to keep me in proximity to a man I need to avoid?

Mary's long thin arm swept out before her in a spokesmodel-worthy arc. "After I show you the spaces we have to work with, I'll introduce you to Nan. That's what everyone has called Cornelia Curry since she became a grandmother."

"I can't wait to meet her."

"Momma, packpack, pease."

Hannah took the pack and settled on the floor. Pride and relief bloomed with her daughter's good behavior. While the two women talked and marked off areas with tape on the floor, Hannah arranged her collection of dolls in a circle and had a pretend tea party with her "circle" snacks.

An hour later, Mary walked back to Eighteenth Street with Tess and Hannah. "My husband, Victor, and I live just one street over on Magnolia Lane. It's going to be so convenient that you're living next door to Nan."

"Yes, lucky." *Except for the delicious temptation of her grandson.*

The Curry house stood proud and regal against a cloudless blue sky, towering over the small Craftsman beside it. Regardless of how wary she was about spending time with Anson, she couldn't wait to see inside his house.

"We go home, Momma?"

"Not yet, sweetie. We're going to go in that big white house and meet Chief Curry's grandmother."

"My chief house?" She put her tiny hand over her star badge, ran ahead of them and up the front steps.

"Your daughter has really good motor and language skills," Mary said. "I have a younger cousin with Down syndrome. When he was little, he struggled with both."

"We've been lucky compared to many, in those two respects. But her success has also been in part to a ton of physical and speech therapy."

A young woman with long dark hair and ivory skin answered their knock.

"Good afternoon, Jenny," Mary said. "I'd like you to meet Tess and her adorable daughter, Hannah."

"Welcome. You're the ones that just moved into Anson's house next door."

"That's us." Tess accepted her hand.

"Come inside, please."

A massive cherrywood staircase curved along one side of the foyer leading to discoveries Tess longed to explore.

Mary hung her cardigan on an antique coatrack beside a man's brown leather jacket. Tess stopped herself just before leaning in to see if it smelled like the man who teased her desires. A pair of sturdy work boots sat beside a small pair of ladies' shoes.

Add a pair of child's shoes and... Stop it! She squeezed her eyes closed and forced down the longing to see such a sight in her own home. *Damn the man for making me dream of things that I shouldn't.*

"I have a cousin about your age," Jenny said to Hannah.

The young woman's voice brought Tess back to reality.

Jenny knelt to Hannah's level, a kind and honest smile on her face. "Maybe she can come over to play sometime."

"Play toys?"

Her daughter's voice rang with excitement. A playdate would be great, if the other child accepted Hannah's differences.

"My cousin, Katie, loves toys." Jenny held out a hand and Hannah took it. "Nan is in the back sunroom. Come with me." She led them through the old family home.

Tess had become really good at taking a person's measure by the way they reacted to Hannah. Sometimes it was in the way they smiled or didn't smile. The eyes were particularly telling. And how they treated her daughter over time was the true measure of their character. Jenny's big, hazel eyes had softened with an inner warmth you couldn't fake.

I like this girl.

They entered an elegantly appointed sunroom overlooking the back porch and yard. The tiny lady sitting on a maroon velvet sofa had her head turned as she stared out the window. Her silver-white hair was braided and twined into a bun at the back of her head. She looked as antique as the items surrounding her.

"Good afternoon, Nan," Mary said cheerfully. "I've brought some lovely ladies to meet you."

Anson's grandmother slid glasses farther up on her nose and studied Tess with faded blue eyes. "I'm Cornelia Annette West Curry, but everyone calls me Nan. And you're my new neighbors. I saw you out the window this morning."

"Yes, ma'am. I'm Tess Harper. And this is my daughter, Hannah Lynn. I'm here to help set up the Oak Hollow museum. I've been told you'll be a great help with the history."

Hannah let go of her mother's hand, skipped over to Nan and touched her wrinkled arm. "You old."

"Hannah," Tess scolded as her cheeks warmed with a scarlet blush.

Nan smiled at the little girl before her. "You're right. I'm *very* old, and that's why I know all the history and juicy town stories."

Hannah stroked the tissue paper skin on the back of Nan's hand. "Soft."

Tess pressed two fingers to her forehead and ducked her head. "If now isn't a good time, we can come back later."

Nan patted Hannah's cheek. "Now is just as good as any. I don't do much lately."

Mary motioned for Tess to step a few feet away. "Nan hasn't smiled like that since her stroke. I think being around your little girl might be good for her.

Get acquainted while I slip into her kitchen and make tea."

Tess turned to see her daughter sitting on the velvet sofa beside the fragile little woman. Both heads were bent over a thick book.

"What color is that flower?" Nan asked.

"Wed," Hannah cheered. "We make flowers?"

"It's getting close to wintertime, but maybe we can plant some flowers in my greenhouse. Pansies are good in the winter."

Her daughter's face beamed, and she returned to studying the pictures in the book.

This lady they'd just met was more tender and accepting of her child than her paternal grandmother ever would've been. Tess's chest tightened with a familiar longing for family. One she worked very hard to keep buried.

"Have a seat," Nan said, and pointed to an over-stuffed chair.

The soft cushions molded to fit her curves as she allowed herself to relax. "What are you two reading?"

"Flower book, Momma."

"It's one of my many gardening books."

"I noticed your garden from my side porch. Looks like you put a lot of work into it." The second Nan glanced toward the windows and sighed, Tess feared she'd said something wrong.

"I used to work out there every day." Her thin hands folded together against her chest.

Hannah slid off the couch and went over to a shelf of porcelain birds, this time making her mother proud when she clasped her little hands behind her back and studied the fragile figurines. "No hand, Momma. Eyes only."

"Good girl, sweetie."

Nan's moment of melancholy disappeared, and she chuckled. "You have a well-behaved child. You must be a good mother."

"Thank you. I try."

"Where are you from? Who are your people?"

"I was born in San Diego. My dad was in the Navy and we moved around until I was nine. Then my father joined the San Diego police department. After we lost him, my mother, brother and I moved to Boston. That's where I fell in love with history."

"Married?"

"No, ma'am. Not anymore."

"Harper is your ex-husband's name?"

Bile threatened to rise in her throat. "No. I took back my maiden name."

"Couldn't stand the sound of his?"

"Something like that." *He didn't even want his own child to have his last name. Bastard.*

"That's how I felt about my first husband." Nan reopened the book as Hannah crawled onto the sofa beside her. "He died in the war, shortly after we were married. A few months with that man was more than enough to show me I'd made a big mistake." She touched her jaw as if remembering an old injury.

"Probably killed by his own men. But I proudly kept my second husband's name." Her gaze turned to a grouping of framed photographs on the side table. A faraway, dreamy look hinted at the girl in love she'd once been. "Isaac was the father of my children and love of my life."

"Anson's grandfather?"

"That's right. He was also the chief of police many years ago. Then mayor."

Tess leaned forward and studied the photos. Her eyes lingered on one of Anson standing tall and gorgeous in dress blues.

"Handsome, isn't he?"

She jerked her gaze away from his image. "They all are." The other woman's grin told her she hadn't been as private with her thoughts as she'd hoped.

"What do you think of my grandson?"

"He seems like a great chief of police."

"And?" Mischief twinkled in Nan's eyes.

Butterflies started up a raucous dance as a blush warmed her skin, and she prayed the temptation wasn't obvious on her face. She was saved from lying or redirecting the conversation when her daughter popped up in her face like a jack-in-the-box.

"Momma, I hungry."

Mary entered as if on cue and set a full tray on the coffee table. "Did I hear that someone wants to eat? How about some afternoon tea and cookies?"

Tess smoothed down Hannah's static-filled curls. "Look, sweetie. A real tea party."

Her daughter radiated joy, making everyone smile. "I like cookie."

"Me, too," Nan said. "My favorite are shortbread. What's your favorite, Hannah?"

"All cookies." Her little arm swept out in an all-encompassing motion, and she sat on the floor beside the coffee table. "I bake."

"That's right," Tess said. "We have lots of fun baking."

"Anson's favorite are double chocolate chip." A gleam brightened Nan's expression.

"We make cookies for my chief, Momma?"

"I think we can find some time for that."

Mary poured tea and gave Hannah hers in a small, elegant demitasse cup. "Nan, tell her about the antique baker's cabinet that belonged to your mother."

Nan accepted her own cup. "I have such fond memories of that simple time in my life."

"I'd love to hear your stories and put a personal touch on the museum exhibits." Tess pulled a journal from her purse and took notes as the older woman reminisced about growing up in Oak Hollow.

Tess's only challenge was keeping her gaze from drifting back to the photograph of Chief Anson Curry.

Chapter Four

After pancakes at the charming Acorn Cafe, Tess and Hannah made their way across the shady center of the town square. The crisp morning breeze brought the scent of a wood fire and the earthy tang of dried leaves crunching underfoot. Goose bumps pebbled Tess's skin as she drew close to the Oak Hollow Police Station.

Why am I nervous? I've got to stop letting myself think of Anson as someone I want in my life. Or in my bed.

"Momma, I see my chief?" Hannah hopped onto the sidewalk and tiptoed along a wavy crack.

"Maybe, but he might be out around town somewhere." She shifted the box of homemade "thank-you" cookies and couldn't decide if she wanted him to be there or not. The last time she'd seen him, he hadn't smiled at her, or even talked much. That he didn't think of her in the same way she did him was obvious.

The inside of the police department wasn't anything like the big city station where her dad had worked. It still offered the expected coffee aroma but had a small-town, welcoming atmosphere. Potted plants and watercolor landscapes mixed in with metal office furniture that looked too new for the old, brick building. Her stomach flipped at the sight of Anson sitting at a large desk behind a glass wall.

"Good morning, ladies."

The deep voice jerked her gaze to the reception counter and Officer Walker's perceptive grin. "Good morning."

"Cookies," Hannah squealed and bounced from foot to foot. "For you. For my chief."

Tess offered the box. "A small thank-you for helping us move in."

"Thanks." He took the goodies and smiled at Hannah. "Do I have to share them with Chief Curry?"

"Share nice." Hannah wagged her finger like a mother scolding a naughty child.

His chuckle was deep and friendly. "Yes, ma'am. Let's see if he wants one."

"Oh, maybe…" Before Tess could finish saying they shouldn't bother him, he came out from behind the counter and headed for Anson's office with her daughter on his heels.

"Chief, you have visitors bearing goodies."

Anson looked up from an open folder and grinned at Hannah peering over the edge of his desk. "Thank you, little one. I was just thinking that I need a snack." His smile shifted down a few notches when he looked at Tess.

She caught the flash of guarded wariness that darkened his blue eyes before he refocused on her beaming child.

"I need to get back to the front desk." Walker grabbed a cookie and pointed it at his boss. "They're for *both* of us. Miss Hannah said we have to share."

Tess inhaled, but the vain attempt to settle her nerves was a joke. "Hannah, we better get going and let Chief Curry get back to work."

"No go, pease."

The phone on his desk rang. "I need to take this call. It's the mayor. Can you wait a couple of minutes?"

"We'll wait out here." She picked up her child and stepped out of his office. Staying was a bad idea, but Hannah would be upset if she didn't get a minute to talk to him.

A lady with a gray pixie cut stood with her back to them as she talked to Officer Walker. "I see we have a new member of the 'Pantie Posse' delivering tempting treats to our fearless leader."

Embarrassment slammed Tess in a hot wave.

Oh my God, no. This is not happening. That's so not what our delivery is.

Still holding her child, she turned to leave, whacked her knee on a chair and hissed through her teeth. A fiery pain shot through her leg. Hannah wiggled to get down, making her stumble and grab the wall to keep them upright.

Officer Walker cleared his throat, and the woman spun around with an "oops" expression across her face.

"No go, Momma."

Even with Hannah fussing and her knee throbbing, she kept walking, right out onto the safety of the sidewalk.

Why did I let Nan and Hannah talk me into taking cookies to him?

"Hannah Lynn, he's very busy keeping everyone safe. Maybe he'll be home when we go over to talk to Nan this evening."

"See Nan?"

"Yes. She's going to show us some more old pictures and tell us another story about when she was a little girl. I have a fun idea. Before we go work at the museum, let's stop in the park for ten minutes."

Smiling, Hannah bounced. "Swing?"

"Yes, but when we go to Momma's work, you have to play nicely with your dolls."

As Tess pushed her daughter on the swing, she rubbed her throbbing knee and wished for an ice pack. Too bad not much could be done for the embarrassment. It took considerable effort, but she managed not to even glance toward the police station. Anson's attitude suddenly made more sense. He already had a whole posse of adoring women. He didn't need her moony-eyed attention.

Thankful to be home after a trying day, Anson unlocked his front door. A stolen car and a drug-related arrest were out of character for his quiet town. Not to mention his distracted state of mind ever since Tess and Hannah stopped by with a batch of his favorite cookies, just like a wife and child might've done. He'd hated to admit his disappointment when they'd rushed away, but the mystery of their sudden departure would have to wait. All he wanted was to take off his boots, crack open a cold beer and focus on something other than the tempting woman next door.

Nan's laugh brought him to a stop in the entry with one hand reaching for his boot heel. It was a sound he'd been trying to coax out of his grandmother for months. Her chuckle was followed by a childish giggle, and goose bumps popped up on his skin.

Hannah's here. Which means, Tess is here to continue messing with my senses.

Avoiding all the squeaky spots in the old oak floor, he walked through the house, not wanting to interrupt whatever had brought joy to Nan. He peeked into the sunroom just as Tess tossed her hair over her shoulder. Her full mouth pulled into a beautiful smile that tugged something in his chest, and he swallowed against the catch in his throat.

She bent her head to write in the notebook on her lap. His grandmother's voice pulled his attention to the sofa, where Hannah sat tucked against her side with a photo album on their laps. The sweet scene made his chest tighten in a different way. A paternal way.

"Anson, come in, dear. I'm just telling Tess about some of the items for the museum. I'm so happy she wants to include stories along with the displays."

"That's great." He did his best to keep his gaze from drifting back to Tess. "Hello again, Hannah."

"He my chief," she told Nan, and patted the star pinned on her purple shirt.

His grandmother's smile was infectious. He moved farther into the room and put a hand on her walker. "Did you get some exercise in today?"

"I did. I need to get my strength back so Hannah and I can go out to the greenhouse and plant some flowers."

Wow. Who knew all it would take is a child to get her living again.

Tess closed her notebook and stood. "We'll get out of your way."

"You two are staying for supper," Nan announced. "A neighbor brought over a big casserole and salad, and we'd love the company."

Tess's eyes flicked briefly to Nan, then Hannah, and ended on him.

He was well acquainted with the wariness in her narrowed gaze. But if having them around would keep Nan smiling, he'd deal with the desire Tess fired off like mini explosions inside him. "Stay and eat with us."

"We stay," Hannah affirmed with a round of clapping.

"Good." Nan obviously believed the matter was settled. "Tess, would you please help Anson put the casserole in the oven to warm and get out the salad? Hannah and I will be just fine right here."

Now he knew what Nan was up to. Matchmaking. But he couldn't bear to disagree when her will to get better had returned. He wasn't ready to let her slip away. A day didn't exist that he'd be ready for that outcome.

"I can handle it by myself," Tess said. "I'm sure Anson would like to relax after work."

The sharp look from his grandmother told him what move he'd better make next.

Great. Being alone with a woman I want, who doesn't want me, won't be hard at all. Evil laughter rang in his head. "Kitchen is this way."

The walls of the hallway seemed to be closing in. Even though he couldn't see her, he could feel her behind him. And wanted nothing more than to turn and pull her into his arms, see how she'd fit against him and how her lips tasted. Tess ran into his back, and he realized he'd abruptly stopped. "Sorry," he said, without turning around.

Her hands stayed on his back a moment longer before sliding away. "It's okay. I was moving...too fast."

Her husky whisper shot directly to his groin. He paused a moment longer and then continued toward the kitchen. "If you'll preheat the oven, I'll get stuff out of the fridge."

At this rate, I might need to climb into the freezer!

Tess pressed a hand to her fluttering stomach and forced herself not to reach out and touch him again. When they entered the kitchen, she couldn't hold in a gasp. "This room is beautiful. Original white Shaker cabinets, Carrara marble, apron front sink, and..." His half grin made her stop the verbal list. "I get a little excited about well-preserved history."

"Nice to know what excites you." His eyes widened, then he quickly ducked his head behind the refrigerator door.

Her sweater suddenly felt too heavy against her heated skin. He'd tried to hide his reaction but hadn't been quick enough to cover up his awareness of his suggestive comment. *If he only knew, it's him that's reawakened something inside me.* She turned her attention to the white Viking range and set it to preheat.

"What college degree does someone earn for the work you do?" he asked.

Glad for the change of subject, she happily answered. "I have a degree in history, minors in archeology and art, and a master's in archival science. I was about to go for my doctorate when I got pregnant with Hannah."

"Wow. That's a lot of school."

"I like learning." *And I'd like to learn what turns you on.* Panic struck her square in the gut. Had she said that aloud?

He didn't react, so she released a thank-goodness breath. How could she live next door to this man and his direct line to her libido?

He put a foil-covered glass dish on the stovetop. "This is some chicken dish. It's one of Nan's favorites."

"Do you think she'll give me a tour of this house sometime?"

"I can show you around while the food heats."

"Please stop me if I'm being too nosy."

"Being a cop, I'm pretty nosy myself. You might want to check out the butler's pantry through that door."

While they waited for the oven to reach the desired temperature, Tess explored every inch of the kitchen. Several columns of measurements were written on the inside of the butler's pantry wall. She traced a finger along the height marks under Anson's name. "Hard to believe you were ever this little. Did you grow up in this house?"

"I did." With the toe of his boot, he tapped the bottom of the door frame on the opposite side. "And my little sister, Carol."

The oven dinged its readiness. Once the casserole was heating, they peeked in on Hannah and Nan, who were still reading and appeared content.

"What part of the house do you want to see first?" Anson asked.

"Any areas of the house you're willing to show me. I wouldn't mind even getting a look in the attic." His deep chuckle sent a shiver rippling through her.

"Follow me." He led her up a back staircase to the attic, then hung back silently watching as she meticulously took in every detail.

She stood in the center of the peaked roof structure, overflowing with furniture in need of refinishing, boxes and trunks, and cloth-draped mysteries. The large space was a historian's playground, filled with treasures and stories awaiting discovery.

Once they were back on the second floor, they explored an upstairs parlor turned media room, two bathrooms and four bedrooms. Along the way, their tension morphed into a sort of edgy friendship. On their way back toward the stairs, Tess trailed her fingers across each glass doorknob, her distorted reflection wavering as she moved. How many people had walked this floor and turned these knobs? She could almost hear their voices echoing along the corridor.

"Didn't you say this house has always been in your family?"

"Yep. Curry family home since the day it was built." He opened the last door. "This one is my bedroom."

They stepped into a room he'd skipped on their first pass through the second floor. The air between them heated further.

Was he hesitant to bring me in here, or saving it for last on purpose? No! Don't go there.

"I think most of my furniture is old," he said.

"You're right." The curved lines of art deco pieces were polished to a high gleam and smelled faintly of lemon polish. A wooden tray on the dresser held spare change, several knives and military dog tags. "You were a soldier?"

"Marine. MP." He stepped closer and emptied the contents of his pockets into an empty section of the tray.

The intimacy of the simple act, and his unique, snowy-pine-forest scent had her head swimming. She backed into the bedside table and a lamp tipped.

In a split second, he caught it in one hand, and palmed the small of her back in the other.

Her breath snagged on inhale, and before she could think better of it, she clutched his belt. The pressure increased on her back as Anson's head dipped slightly.

The timer on her phone chimed, startling both of them.

She stepped back to a safe distance and pulled out the intrusive piece of technology. "Dinner. It's ready. We should…go down."

Oh good grief. I sound like a blithering idiot.

The four of them sat around an ornate, Colonial Revival dining room table big enough for twelve people. They talked of everyday things, and Hannah proudly used her best manners. This was how Tess had envisioned raising her child—sharing meals, conversation about the day and her daughter's laughter.

Nan dabbed her mouth with a cloth napkin. "I called Jenny while you two were upstairs. She agreed it's a great idea for Hannah to spend the day with us tomorrow so Tess can get some work done at the museum. If it's okay with you, of course?"

Tess was shocked by the offer. "She can be a lot to handle. I don't want you to overdo it and tire yourself out."

"I love having a little one around. Makes me feel younger. After watching her dance about the yard as you moved in, I remembered what it was to feel that free. I walked five laps around the house today. Jenny practically had to run to keep up with me."

Anson studied his grandmother, then turned to Tess. "Having Hannah here seems to be what Nan needs to get moving again. I can vouch for Jenny being good with kids."

"Hannah Lynn, would you like to stay here tomorrow while I work at my new job?"

"Yes. I stay." Another bite of food disappeared into her mouth.

"Wonderful." Nan pushed her empty plate forward. "She can help Jenny and me put out the rest of the Halloween decorations."

"I appreciate the help. I'll only be a few blocks away if you should need me."

Nan chuckled. "I'm very familiar with how close we are to the square."

"Oh, of course you are." Tess's cheeks warmed, and she made the mistake of looking at Anson. His big grin only made her skin flame hotter. She grabbed her and Hannah's empty plates. "I'll clean up before we head home."

"Anson will help you while I read one more story to Hannah," Nan declared.

Tess helped Anson clean the kitchen while Nan read to Hannah from an old copy of *Children's Classic Fairy Tales*. By the time they'd finished cleaning —and dancing around their attraction by sticking to work-related conversation—Hannah was sound asleep on the couch.

Tess sat beside her and stroked her head. "I need to get her home and into bed."

"Jenny is here by seven o'clock every morning, and my old bones wake up with the sun. Bring Hannah over as early as you need to." Nan's fingers drummed on the arm of the sofa. "Anson, carry this little angel and make sure they get home safely."

"I don't need any help." Tess jumped to her feet.

"Better let me help. If you don't, I'll be in trouble and might not get dessert tomorrow," he teased.

For Nan's sake, Tess surrendered control. "Can't have that. Thank you again for supper. See you in the morning, Mrs. Curry."

"You will call me Nan, just like everyone else."

"All right then. Sleep well, Nan."

"Good night, dear."

He gently scooped Hannah into his arms and cuddled her against his chest. "Let's get you home, little one." His voice was pitched low and soothing.

Tess's heart did two things in a split second. It broke for the father her daughter didn't have and melted at the tenderness Anson showed a child he hardly knew.

They stepped out onto the front porch, and she hurried ahead of him, thinking it best not to linger on the sight of her daughter in his arms. The brisk night air chilled her skin, making her shiver as she unlocked their front door and held it open for Anson to step through, with her whole world in his arms.

"Straight to bed or do you need to wake her to take a bath?" he whispered.

"To bed. The bath can wait." Tess led him into the yellow bedroom and pulled back the covers before he laid Hannah on the mattress. She couldn't take her eyes off his hand and how big it looked gently stroking the crown of her daughter's head.

"Sweet dreams, little one," he said, and stepped out of the room.

She took off Hannah's shoes and jeans, then tucked her in for the night. With a bolstering breath, she braced herself for being alone with her fantasy man.

He stood in the center of the living room, looking around like he'd never seen his own house. She followed Anson's gaze to the built-in shelves she'd filled with precious and painful memories. Things she wasn't ready to share with him. Before he could ask any questions, she opened the front door.

"Even though we were coerced, thank you for carrying her home. And for the house tour." Their "moment" in his bedroom flashed before her. *Damn, why'd I bring that up?*

"Anytime." Anson's blue-eyed gaze danced with amusement before he ducked his head and stepped outside. "Sleep well, Tess."

Fat chance of that.

She closed the door to prevent herself from watching him walk away. Tonight, Anson hadn't treated her indifferently like before, and in fact, seemed to be fighting his own temptations. Part of the time shutters would fall over his eyes as he distanced himself, then she'd blink and he'd wear his devil's grin, drawing her in with flirtation. Maybe he wasn't as immune to their attraction as she'd thought.

"I can't figure you out, Chief Anson Curry. But why am I even bothering?"

Chapter Five

Hannah ran ahead of Tess and up the steps of Anson and Nan's house. "Momma, what that sound?"

As Tess got closer, the whining of baby animals came from a cardboard box by the front door. "Sounds like puppies."

"Puppy!" Hannah shrieked and knelt beside the box.

She joined her and stroked the head of one of three fluffy pups. "Where did you little fellows come from?"

The front door opened and Anson stepped out. "What do you have there?"

She shivered as she always did when first seeing him. "They were here when we walked up."

With a large hand, he reached in and scooped up a puppy. "Looks like they might be part German shepherd."

His nearness made her want to lean in and pull away all at the same time. "Does this kind of thing happen often?"

"People leaving animals on my doorstep?" He held the tiny pup in front of his face and it licked his nose. "More than it should. Somehow, I've become the person who'll find homes for all the strays or unwanted animals. I even had someone bring me a baby squirrel."

"What did you do with it?"

"Took it to the wildlife rescue on the edge of town. These babies barely have their eyes open."

"Does that mean they'll need to be bottle-fed?"

"Yes, but I know someone whose dog just had a litter. Maybe she'll adopt and nurse these babies." He put the dog into Hannah's arms.

"My puppy." Hannah cuddled the whining and wiggling baby.

Regret seeped into Tess's heart. "Sweetie, we can't have a puppy right now. We'll be moving soon. Probably into an apartment that might not let us have a pet. Once we get a house of our own we can get one."

"He wuvs me."

Tess blinked against tears and stroked the little dog in her daughter's arms. "I know, sweetie. Animals always love you."

The puppy settled on his back in the little girl's lap and stretched out his legs.

Anson knelt beside them and tickled the happy animal's tummy. "What do you think about sharing him? You can come over and visit him anytime you want."

Hannah cocked her head as if considering the proposal.

Tess cleared her throat and crooked her finger. Trusting a man to do what he said was something she had a hard time with.

He grinned sheepishly and followed her a few steps away. "Guess that was the wrong thing to say?"

"You can't make that promise to her if you don't really intend to keep the dog. Besides, we won't be here much longer and—" She lost her breath when he tucked hair behind her ear.

"Tess, I wouldn't promise something to a child, or anyone, and not mean it. My old dog died six months ago, and I've been planning to get another."

She wanted to believe he was a man who was true to his word. Such men existed, but her focus couldn't be sidelined in the pursuit of a romance, especially since they'd only be here for a short time. Pesky tears stung the backs of her eyes. "I just don't want her to get too attached and be hurt when we leave."

Am I talking about attachment to the animal or the man?

His hand rose in what looked like a Boy Scout

salute. "I'll make sure she knows he's mine, and I'll take good care of him."

"I don't know if you saw, but the puppy you put in her arms has one deformed back leg. And trust me, she'll know if you choose a different dog."

"I noticed the pup's leg. He needs love just like the others do. From my experience, he'll adapt and be fine." The breeze ruffled Anson's hair as he turned and walked back to Hannah.

Words momentarily escaped her. He was so different from Brent or any of the guys she'd dated. He appeared to have qualities a real man should have, but she'd been burned by first impressions before.

Can he really be such a good guy?

Hannah's giggle refocused Tess's attention. She joined them to see the baby sucking on her little finger.

"It tickle. Momma. My chief puppy. I visit."

"That's great." She caught Anson's gaze and smiled. "I don't know what you said to her, but good job."

"Maybe you'll end up liking this town enough that you'll want to come back and visit now and then."

There was truth in his statement. Tess liked this town and its citizens a little more every day.

A crisp, fall wind blew through the town square playground and fluttered the wisps of hair falling from Tess's ponytail. She sipped coffee from a paper cup and waved at Hannah as she slid down the slide, then ran around to climb the playscape again. With Nan and Jenny watching Hannah most of the day, she'd gotten a ton of work done at the museum. Now it was playtime before they headed home to make dinner.

"What's up, neighbor?"

Tess jumped at the sound of Anson's deep voice coming over her shoulder. "Jeez, you startled me. You must be good at sneaking up on criminals."

"I've been known to catch a few." His arm brushed hers and she flinched. "What's got you so jumpy? Have you broken the law?"

"None that I know of." *Other than the off-limits, getting-you-naked fantasies I can't seem to stop myself from having.*

"My friend's dog accepted the puppies you found on my porch. Once they're big enough, I'll bring my little guy home and find families for the others."

"That's good news." Hannah was out of view, and she shifted her stance to try and see her. "I hate that closed-in section at the top of the slide. I try not to be an overprotective mother, but I can't see her when she's in there."

The second the words left her mouth, Hannah's high-pitched scream filled the air. Tess dropped her coffee and ran. Anson's long strides pulled ahead of her, and he vaulted up and over the side of the structure just as Tess scrambled up the slide. She barely noticed smacking her forehead on the lip of the plastic tunnel. They converged from two directions just in time to witness one of her biggest nightmares come true.

"You're a monster," said a little boy, and sank his teeth into Hannah's back.

Her baby's fearful cries pierced her heart. She pulled her away from the hateful attack and into her arms.

"Tommy Seaton," Anson roared. "Get over here! Now!"

The mean little boy froze and turned startled eyes on the chief of police. "I… I didn't do anything."

Tess cradled her crying daughter, rocking and murmuring soothing words. "It's okay, my sweet girl. Momma's here."

"I saw everything." Anson's words were delivered with barely restrained fury, and his stern expression didn't leave room for argument.

The boy's face blanched as he glanced nervously between the crying little girl and the police officer's formidable stare. "Are you going to put me in jail?"

"I'm thinking about it. Where's your father?"

The kid tugged at the collar of his dirty shirt and shrugged. "Don't know."

Anson scooted backward, rose from his crouched position and pointed back the way he'd come. "Follow me. Now."

The boy glanced once more at Tess and Hannah, cast his eyes down, then did as Anson ordered.

They both disappeared from view, but she could

hear him doling out guilt inducing words to the mean-spirited child.

Good luck reforming that little hooligan.

Another man's voice joined the conversation. "What'd I tell you about runnin' off? Get in the truck before I tan your hide a good one."

Hannah tipped her sweet, cherub face up to her mother. "W-w-why, Momma?"

Her trembling lower lip and pleading eyes almost gutted Tess. *What do I say? How can I take away her pain and confusion?* She wiped Hannah's tears and ignored the ones trickling down her own cheeks. "My sweet girl, he's just a mean little boy. You didn't do anything wrong."

Hannah's breath shuddered. "I not monster."

Tess's throat burned as she choked on a restrained sob, and a sharp lash of anguish branded her heart. "Beautiful girl, you are definitely *not* a monster. That little boy is probably just excited about Halloween tomorrow. Maybe he's dressing up in a monster costume."

"He bad. Hurt me."

"I'm so sorry, sweetie. Let me see your back." She raised her purple shirt and sucked in a breath. Three sets of teeth marks marred the beautiful, soft skin of her tiny back. Even through clothing he'd almost drawn blood. Unable to bear the sight any longer, she lowered the shirt and shame gushed in. *How could I have let this happen to my baby?* She tucked her daughter's head in the crook of her neck and held her close.

"Tess?" Anson's voice was low and soothing. "Is she okay?" He crawled into the small space on hands and knees.

She covered her mouth, fearful she'd burst into hysterical tears if she spoke. With trembling fingers, she raised the back of Hannah's shirt.

His eyes sparked and a muscle twitched in his jaw. "Let's get her home."

Hannah turned to Anson and leaned forward to touch his badge. "Star and circle. Safe?"

He took her hand gently in his, swallowed hard and cleared his throat. "I do want to keep you safe. I'm sorry I didn't get here before he hurt you."

"He gone?"

"Yes. He's gone," Anson said. "Ready to go home?"

She sniffled and nodded.

Tess maneuvered around and, with her child in her lap, they went down the slide. He met them at the bottom and helped pull her to her feet. Hannah wrapped her arms and legs around her mother and clung like a little monkey.

Anson touched a finger to the tender place on her forehead and his eyes asked the question he probably didn't want Hannah to hear.

Even the slight brush of his finger was uncomfortable. She repressed a hiss and retreated a step. "I'm fine. Just a little bump."

He looked like he wanted to argue, but only put a hand on the small of her back and guided them toward her SUV. Pulling away from his touch was the smart thing to do, but the warmth of his broad hand felt good. She could comfort Hannah all on her own, but had no one to soothe her own hurts.

She cut her gaze to him, surprised to see some of her pain reflected in his eyes. It would be so easy to fall into his embrace, let him share her anguish, support her through this nightmare. But she couldn't risk letting her guard down. Couldn't let herself start depending on him.

I don't need a hero.

Her pulse raced and her steps quickened as she put space between them.

Once Hannah was buckled into her booster seat, Tess tried to open the driver's door, but Anson covered her knuckles with the palm of his hand.

"Let me drive you."

"I can drive my daughter home. It's only a few blocks."

"Tess, you're shaking."

Again, she jerked her hand away. "I don't need you to keep rescuing me. I've been doing this all on my own for over four years. I need to get her home." She got in and started the car. The overly helpful officer stepped back but continued to stand staring at her with his muscled arms crossed over his chest. Arms that could comfort her if…

Stop it, Tess Harper. Get your head in the game.

She pulled out of the parking spot and drove down Main Street. "Are you hungry, sweetie? What should we have for dinner?"

"Taco, pease."

"Good idea. I'm glad we bought crunchy taco shells." She glanced in the mirror and wasn't surprised to see a lump right in the middle of her forehead. No wonder Anson was concerned.

Probably should've thanked him, rather than spitting venom his way.

Anson watched Tess drive away and kicked a stray rock. It rebounded off the curb and almost hit his shin.

"That's one damn stubborn woman."

He turned and headed back to the station, feeling more than a little upset about what had happened to Hannah. And wondering why he continued trying to help a woman who didn't want it. He was doing a terrible job of sticking to his plan to keep his distance. Apparently, self-preservation wasn't his strongest quality.

Why do I repeatedly set myself up for this?

A passing woman shot him a startled look, and he realized he'd growled low in his throat. Anson forced a smile and tipped his cowboy hat. "Evening, Mrs. Suarez."

Walker met him at the station door. "Glad I caught you before you head home."

"What's up?"

"I switched night desk duty with Carter. Hope that's okay?"

"Sure. Hot date tonight?"

"Actually, yes." Walker flashed a toothy grin that looked shockingly white against his olive skin.

"Good for you." *At least someone knows a cooperative female.* "Did you put those papers about the Blue Santa program on my desk?"

"Yep. All they need is your signature." Walker turned for the door but stopped. "I saw you talking to the oldest Seaton brother, then heard him yelling at his kid when he got in his truck. What's that about?"

His teeth ached from clenching, and he wanted to hit something good and hard. "Tommy hurt Hannah on the playground."

Walker let go of the door and his eyes widened. "That sweet little girl that moved into your house."

"Afraid so."

"My sister would have a fit if someone did that to my nephew, Cody. She's become super protective of him ever since he was diagnosed with autism."

"That's understandable." Anson rubbed his eyes in a vain attempt to erase the visual of Tess and Hannah clinging to one another with tears on their cheeks. But he was also bothered by the deep sadness on the little boy's face. "Think I scared the crap out of Tommy."

"Good. Maybe if you keep it up, he won't turn out like his dad and uncles."

"Let's hope, but the men in his life will make that tough."

"If anyone can do it, it's you. Night, Chief."

Once Anson got everything squared away for the evening, he headed home and checked on Nan but couldn't bring himself to tell her what had happened to Hannah. He was still too disturbed and knew his grandmother would be equally upset. After changing out of his uniform, he went next door, hoping he wasn't setting himself up for more verbal abuse, but he had to check on Hannah. And if he was honest, he wanted to check on Tess, too.

He climbed his—*their*—front steps, testing the sturdiness of the railing as he went. A few seconds after he knocked, Hannah's face appeared in the window, followed by a delighted squeal.

"My chief, Momma. My chief here."

"My hands are full," Tess called out. "Let him in, please."

The door flew open and she bounced on bare feet in a pair of pink pajamas.

"Hey there, little one. Mind if I come in?"

"I took bath. Momma cook tacos." She grabbed his hand and dragged him into the kitchen, where Tess was draining hamburger meat. After circling him three times, Hannah ran down the hall to her room.

Tess still hadn't looked at him so he cleared his throat. "Sorry to interrupt your dinner. I just wanted to check on her. Glad to see she's back to her happy self."

The cast-iron skillet clanged as she returned it to the burner and added water. "Have you eaten?"

"No. Are you asking me to stay?"

"Hannah will want you to." She tore open a seasoning packet with too much force and only half of the orange powder made it onto the meat. "Shoot fire and save matches."

He didn't dare laugh or even smile at her mishap or quirky exclamation. This intriguing woman was dangerous to his self-control, but she sure did entertain him. The bump on her head was starting to show the first signs of bruising and he wanted to pull her into his arms and kiss it better, but he retained a safe distance and leaned a hip on the soapstone counter. "What about you? Can you bear my company?"

"Stay." She finally met his eyes, but her face was tight with tension and a mother's pain. "It's the least I can do to thank you for your help when…" Her voice trailed off like she couldn't bear to speak about what had happened at the park.

"No need for thanks."

Hannah ran in and put coloring books and a box of crayons on the kitchen table, then pointed at Anson. "Sit."

"Yes, ma'am." He did as ordered, happy to see the biting incident hadn't affected her as much as it had the adults. "What are we doing?"

She looked at him like it was outrageous that he didn't know. "Art."

"Oh, of course." Before he knew it, he was directed to color a picture of an elephant under a palm tree, but his choice of crayon color was questioned.

"Not purple."

"How about red?" He couldn't help but chuckle as curls danced around her rosy cheeks and her finger wagged in his face.

"Not wed."

"Blue?"

"Fine." She dragged out the word, shook her head, then went back to coloring flowers with a pink crayon.

He had one elephant ear colored when Hannah sighed. "What's wrong? Is pink not the right color for your flowers?"

"Not lines." Her finger poked at the spots she'd colored outside the black borders.

Anson returned to his page and colored rapidly, with only minor regard for the shape of the elephant. "That's boring. There's nothing wrong with coloring outside the lines now and then. Keeps life interesting."

Hannah giggled and returned to her artwork. "You silly."

Dishes clattered and he glanced at Tess. Her beautiful smile had returned, but it frayed around the edges and her eyes shone misty.

* * *

They ate at the small kitchen table and kept the conversation light and happy. After dinner, Hannah announced he would be reading *Barnyard Dance* and her mother would read *Goodnight Moon*. He glanced at Tess to make sure he was allowed to say yes to the request. With her somewhat reluctant nod of approval, he followed Tess and Hannah into the yellow bedroom.

"This your side." The pint-size cutie patted her bed. "Momma that side."

Déjà vu, or something more like a daydream, hit as he took his assigned book and place on the bed. He'd thought he'd be doing this very thing in this exact room...with his own child. He pulled himself together while Tess read the classic story he remembered from his childhood. When it was his turn, he put on a happy face. This evening was all about making Hannah forget what had happened in the park. Making her feel happy, and safe.

"*Barnyard Dance* by Sandra Boynton." He opened the board book, and while he read the words, Hannah made the animal sounds.

When he'd finished and closed the book, Hannah splayed her palm on his chest. "Where star?"

"It's at home. I only wear it on my uniform."

"You wear. You trick-treat. Keep me safe."

Tess inhaled sharply and bit her lip.

Is she asking me to trick-or-treat with her? The protective mother's shocked, agitated expression combined with the child's beaming smile had him tongue-tied.

"Hannah, he probably has things to do tomorrow night. I doubt he has time for trick-or-treating."

She climbed onto her knees and bounced on the bed. "Pease, pease, pease."

Her mother might flay him, but he couldn't resist this little girl. "Yes, I'll go trick-or-treating with you."

"Tank you!"

"Do I have to wear a costume?"

Hannah tapped a finger on her lips. "Yes. Sheriff."

"That's easy enough. You better get under those covers so your momma can tuck you in." *The momma that's glaring at me.* He kissed the top of Hannah's head and moved to the doorway, but he couldn't bring himself to leave. With the doorframe at his back, he watched the rest of their bedtime routine.

Tess pulled a dropper bottle out of the bedside table drawer and measured out a dose. "Open up." Hannah popped her mouth open like a baby bird and swallowed the liquid. She kissed her child's forehead, cheeks and nose. "Good night, sweet girl. Momma loves you."

"Wuv you, Momma."

Anson stepped into the hallway as Tess rose from the bed.

She pulled the door almost closed and motioned for him to follow her into the living room. "You're the first one she's ever asked to join our nightly bedtime routine. Or to go trick-or-treating." She crossed to the front living room windows and stared out into the night.

"I'm honored. What's that medication you gave her?"

"It's for her heart."

A cold wave settled in his chest. "Is she okay?" When she didn't respond, he bit his tongue, deciding not to pry further tonight. It wouldn't hurt him to work on his patience. He moved to the built-ins and studied the photos and flags he'd noticed the last time. "Is this Hannah's father?"

Her whole body jerked and she spun to face him. "What? Where?" Her wide-eyed gaze flicked around as if she expected the grim reaper to materialize at any second.

Whoa. That's one hell of a reaction. "This man in the Navy uniform." He leaned in and read the inscription on the flag's box frame. "Shawn Joseph Harper."

She released a shuddering breath. "That's my brother."

"Now that you say that, I can see the resemblance."

Her maroon-polished fingertips straightened the photo of a police officer and a woman in a red dress. "My parents, Christopher and Beth Harper."

Hannah's last name is Harper. Maybe she's never been married.

"After my dad left the Navy, he joined the San

Diego police force and died in the line of duty." Tess closed her eyes. "Then she died from cancer thirteen years ago."

Echoes of her sorrow hit him in the chest. "I'm sorry. You were young when she died."

"Nineteen. In my first year of college."

Anson swayed forward but thought better of touching her. She was already as jumpy as a cat in a dance hall. "Do you have other family?"

"Some cousins here and there."

Her shrug was no doubt meant to convey nonchalance, but the pain and loneliness were evident. "What about Hannah's father?" The moment it left his mouth, he wished to recall the question, especially when she rounded on him, fire shooting from her eyes.

"She doesn't *have* a father. He couldn't be *bothered* with anything that wasn't perfect." Air hissed between her teeth. "I've been raising her on my own from before she was even born. From the moment we discovered she had Down syndrome." She kept her voice low, but the fury and bone-deep hurt were unmistakable. "That good-for-nothing, mama's boy, son of a…" She broke off and braced a shoulder against the shelf.

He left them?! What a bastard. "Tess, come sit."

She ran her fingers roughly through her hair but didn't take his offered hand. "You don't understand. Hannah's starting to depend on you. What happens when we move to Houston? If she gets too attached, she'll be hurt when we leave."

The word *leave* flashed like a neon sign in his brain, but he pushed that worry away for the moment. "Houston is only four hours away."

"It might as well be a million miles away as far as a child is concerned." Back and forth she paced from the fireplace to the kitchen. Her small, bare feet were squeaking on the wooden floor with each jerky turn.

His stomach tightened. *She has no one.*

"When we got home from the park, I gave her a bath. I needed to wash away…everything. I put ointment on the bites, even though the skin wasn't broken. I told her the little boy only called her a monster because he was thinking about Halloween costumes." Her fists clenched and unclenched, then she stopped moving, eyes burning fever bright. "The heartbreaking expression on her little face will haunt me for the rest of my life. My baby is beautiful and precious. How could anyone be so cruel to call her that?" She locked her gaze with his. "Is that what some people think of her?"

Her voice had dropped to a strained whisper, choked with raw emotion that caused a knot to form in his throat. Not caring how mad she got, or how much it put his own heart at risk, he closed the distance between them. "No one thinks that. Hannah is beautiful, inside and out." He wrapped his arms around Tess.

She braced her hands against his chest and steeled her features. "I don't need to be coddled like a child."

"It's okay to need someone now and then."

Her lips formed a hard line. "But you can't always be around to rescue me and Hannah. And I don't need you to be. I have to be strong. I don't need a knight in shining armor." Fingers curled into the fabric of his flannel shirt, her pushing became tugging until she dropped her forehead on his breastbone. "Ouch." She let go with one hand and gingerly rubbed the swollen knot. A physical reminder of the awful event of the day.

Her pursed pink lips begged for him to press his mouth against hers. Make her soften under his kiss. Make her burn the way he did. "Tess, honey, take the comfort I'm offering."

"Fine." As if she'd heard his thoughts, she grasped his face and captured his mouth.

The kiss was hard, intense... And so sweet. Cradling the back of her head, he sank into the kiss, stroking her tongue and exploring her soft warm mouth. With a shuddering sigh, she relaxed her weight against him and accepted what he offered. And gave what he needed. But when she tugged open the top buttons of his shirt, he pulled back. Anson wanted to pull her into a dance that lasted all night long, but he couldn't take advantage of her in her distressed state. Couldn't bear for their first time to be filled with anger and hurt. When... If he made love to this woman it had to be about only them.

"Tess, stop. We have to stop."

Her expression shifted from dazed to murderous in a split second. She backed away and wrapped her arms around her waist. "Please, go."

"Can we sit for a minute?"

Without another word, she opened the front door and stood there statue-still, not meeting his eyes.

Disappointment tightened his chest as he stepped across the threshold. Still standing on the welcome mat, he turned back to her. "I'll see you and Hannah tomorrow evening for trick-or-treating."

"Only because she'll be disappointed if you don't."

The door closed, almost hitting his knee. His natural tendency was to save her, but she wasn't an abandoned puppy whom he could easily find a home for. Tess Harper was a complicated, beautiful, tough-as-nails, momma bear of a woman. One with the power to crack his plan to be only a friend. One with the power to break his guarded heart wide-open. He sighed and made his way across the driveway between their houses, the night air doing nothing to cool his heated skin. The time for protecting himself had passed somewhere between finding them laughing with Nan and their kiss. The one that had taken all his strength to resist.

Tess braced her palms flat against the door, embarrassment flaming hot as a branding iron on her skin. She felt tricked by Anson. Led into something she thought he'd reciprocate only to have him spin the world out from under her.

"Why the hell did I allow myself to fall for a man's fake charms once again? I know better than this."

The old house was eerily quiet and lonely, but her own set of annoying ghosts quickly emerged to haunt her. Admitting Anson was right to stop her moment of weakness was like eating a lemon. A rotten lemon with green fuzz. Embarrassment was a prickly pill to swallow, but in hindsight she was grateful he'd stopped her from making a horrible mistake. Sleeping with Anson Curry would have been a huge slipup, and one that might have wrecked the job she was here to do.

Rather than reaching for the bottle of red wine on the counter, she opted for a cup of herbal tea. In her current mood, if she started on the alcohol she'd drink the whole bottle and wake with a horrible headache. She jerked open a drawer with too much force and the whole thing came out. She caught it before it hit the floor, but utensils clattered down, barely missing her feet.

"Damn. Maybe I do need the wine."

The old drawer refused to go back on its track. Rubbing the wooden rails with a bar of soap would make things slide smoothly, but that trick of the antique trade would have to wait until she wasn't tempted to smash things with her bare hands. As she placed the half-full drawer on the countertop, she felt a piece of paper stuck underneath. It didn't easily come free so she tipped the drawer to see that it was secured with tape. Leaving it was probably the right thing to do, but curiosity took over and she pulled it free. It was a prescription refill for birth control pills written out to Brenda Curry.

"Why is this hidden? And who is Brenda?" Tess had never met a mystery she didn't long to solve, and even though this one might be none of her business, she knew it would continue to inhabit her mind. "I should stick to tea and forget the mystery solving. Especially ones that involve the name Curry."

Once her mug of water was hot, she dunked a tea bag and concentrated on the liquid growing darker with each mesmerizing swirl.

"I'll finish this job, find a place for us in Houston and then…" Her breath shuddered. "We'll face heart surgery head-on."

Chapter Six

At moonrise on Halloween night, Hannah bounced beside her mother with her empty, plastic pumpkin swinging in a wide arc. "Go, Momma."

"I'm almost ready, sweetie." *But not ready to see Anson.* Tess slipped on a pair of silver ballerina flats, then opened the front door.

"You here," Hannah squealed, and dashed out to stand beside Anson.

Tess came face-to-face with the off-limits fantasy man she couldn't escape. His intense, moody gaze stared out from under the brim of a black, suede cowboy hat. Warmth scalded her skin, and she fought a moment of irrational fear that he'd tapped directly into her fantasies.

She stumbled over the threshold and tugged the hem of her iridescent skirt. The midthigh costume suddenly lacked the needed protection against his heated observation. If he kept looking at her like this, she'd melt into a puddle.

"What? Something wrong?" *I should've dressed as a zombie.*

He rubbed a hand across his brow, shielding his eyes. "Nope. All good. Nan is waiting for this pretty little fairy to come trick-or-treat at our house." After a few seconds of staring down at Hannah's beaming smile, he once again glanced at Tess. "Make that two very beautiful fairies."

Her blood surged and she caught her lip between her teeth, annoyed that she *wanted* to smile at him. And she hadn't missed his pink-tinged cheeks glowing above a perfectly groomed blond beard. At least he seemed as unsettled as she was. Attraction and wariness battled inside her as they descended the steps to the busy sidewalk.

Scary creatures, Disney characters and plenty of witches and ghosts bustled around in a flurry of excited action. The myriad of distractions would *hopefully* make it easier to keep her eyes—and thoughts—off him.

Hannah ran ahead toward Nan and Anson's house and was hugging his grandmother when they caught up.

"Don't you girls look lovely tonight." Nan attempted to rise from the wicker chair but struggled.

Anson rushed to take her arm and helped her to her feet. "I thought Jenny was going to stay with you."

"You worry too much." She patted his cheek, then dropped a handful of goodies into Hannah's pumpkin. "Jenny is in the house opening more bags of candy and will be out at any moment. You two take this lovely little lady trick-or-treating. I'll be just fine right here on my own front porch."

After Tess took photos, the three of them set off along the sidewalk, stopping at every house. Hannah insisted on being in the middle with each of them holding one of her hands, which meant Tess and Anson got to take turns holding her rapidly filling plastic pumpkin. Her other demand was that they wait at the edge of the porches and let her ring the bell all on her own. For the first few houses, Tess and Anson remained silent and awkwardly looking anywhere but at one another.

At house number six, Tess couldn't take another second of tension. "I'm sorry I uhm…jumped on you last night. I realize that's not what you meant for me to do."

His mouth quirked up at one corner, and he hooked both thumbs in his front pockets. "You don't need to apologize for anything. I'm the one that's sorry."

"For what?"

Anson stepped closer and dropped his voice to a whisper. "For not kissing you all night long."

Flutters erupted in her belly, sending waves of heat licking along her skin.

"I couldn't sleep," he continued. "Kept wishing I was...keeping you awake, too."

Before she could even begin to process the tingles shooting through her body or what his confession meant, Hannah took their hands once again. Anson's smile hinted that the conversation was only on pause.

"Go, pease." Hannah tugged them along the sidewalk.

Tess still struggled for speech, but reluctantly gave up on holding back a smile that answered his. *I could've worn a suit of armor and it wouldn't have protected me from him tonight.*

"Circle." Hannah broke away from them and ran to stand beside a large sundial. "Not it." She came back for her pumpkin, then made her way to the door of a red brick Tudor.

"I've seen her do that several times before," he said. "What circle is she looking for?"

"I wish I knew. It's her favorite shape, and she's always looking for some version of it that seems to elude her. I hope I can someday figure it out. But lately, circles are starting to be edged out by stars."

"Because of me?" A tender expression softened his angular features.

"Yep. Didn't you notice the star you gave her is always pinned on her shirt? I keep meaning to ask you for a backup. If this one gets lost or broken, I'm in for some major upset. She'll cry, then I'll cry."

"I'll give you two more, just in case. I can even get my hands on a metal badge."

"She'd love that."

A little boy dressed as a superhero headed toward Hannah.

Tess sucked in a breath. "It's the biter."

"Wait." Anson caught her hand. "He's going to apologize. I had a long talk with Tommy this morning."

Before she could protest or pull away, Tommy cut his eyes to Anson and nodded.

He squeezed her fingers. "Let's move closer but give him a chance to make things right."

The small boy with dark hair—in desperate need of a trim—shifted the lollipop in his mouth. "I'm sorry I was mean to you and hurt you. I promise I won't do it again."

Hannah cocked her head, then smiled at him, and Tess released the breath that had been lodged in her lungs.

Tommy took the lollipop out of his mouth and handed it to Hannah before turning and running away.

"Hannah Lynn, do not put that—"

Her little fairy popped the candy into her mouth before Tess could grab it.

"—into your mouth," she finished unnecessarily. "Great. Germs. That's the last thing I need right now." She gently pulled it from her daughter's mouth.

"Let me hold this while you go to the next house, sweetie."

"Okay, Momma. Stay." Hannah pointed to her mother's feet, then hurried along a winding stone path.

Tess tossed the secondhand candy under a bush and glanced away from her sweet girl long enough to catch sight of Tommy walking by himself. "Anson, is Tommy alone?"

"No. That's his older brother, Jeremy Seaton." He hitched a thumb toward a lanky teenager who couldn't take his eyes off the screen of his cell phone. "They don't have a good home life. I imagine their father is drunk somewhere."

"And their mother?"

"She died a few years ago."

A lump formed in her throat. She knew what it was to lose a parent at an early age. Her heart broke for the brothers, and she felt terrible about her ill thoughts toward Tommy. She waved at her baby girl as she carefully stepped from stone to stone on her way back to the spot where she had demanded Tess wait. "Anson, call Tommy over and see if he wants to trick-or-treat with us."

Anson twisted open a green Jolly Rancher and popped it into his mouth. "I suspected you have a forgiving heart."

"Only for those that deserve it." She winced at the bitterness in her tone, but the thought of granting absolution to Brent and his family cramped her stomach.

"Remind me to stay on your good side," he teased, then walked over to the teen, who flinched and stared wide-eyed at the Chief of Police. Tommy approached them warily, but visibly relaxed when Anson smiled and ruffled his hair.

"Take, Momma," Hannah said.

She took her daughter's candy, bent to her level and pointed to Anson and the boys. "Is it okay if that little boy, Tommy, walks with us? He doesn't have a momma to be with him."

"Yes. He sorry." Without a moment's hesitation, Hannah ran toward Anson and the boys.

Tess followed, pleased her lack of forgiving Hannah's father hadn't rubbed off on her sweet child. She gave her friendliest smile to the small boy, who stared at her with wary eyes. "We'd like it if you'd trick-or-treat with us."

Tommy glanced at Anson, and after receiving a nod of approval, he smiled shyly and fell into step beside them. The older brother hung back several paces, no doubt not wanting to be seen with a police officer. Bit by bit, Tommy relaxed and seemed to be enjoying himself. He even took Hannah's hand to help her up a set of stairs. Tess captured the unexpected moment with her camera and hoped the sad little boy was having fun.

"I have to go out of town tomorrow morning,"

Anson said while they waited at the edge of one porch.

A surge of disappointment surprised her, but she stuffed it down. It was an unacceptable reaction to his leaving. "Where are you going?"

"International Association of Chiefs of Police annual conference."

"That's a mouthful. Do you go every year?"

"Yes. I was going to cancel this time, but Nan insisted I go. It'll only be for two nights. Friday and Saturday then home late on Sunday. Jenny is staying with her, but…" Deep grooves formed between his brows.

"But you're still worried?"

"A bit. The last time I went out of town is when she had her stroke."

"I'll be happy to check in on her. Hannah is scheduled to be with Jenny and Nan part of the day tomorrow, unless you think it's too much for her to deal with while you're away?" His full watt smile disarmed her and she swayed closer, hoping to catch a whiff of his woodsy scent.

"Hannah has been really good for Nan. You should definitely let her stay with them."

The children returned from the door, and they resumed their trek through the neighborhood. Once their candy buckets were brimming full, the boys left to find their father.

Worried about Hannah's lagging pace and labored breathing, Tess picked her up, the stress on her daughter's heart striking fear in her own. "Are you ready to go home?"

"No yet, Momma."

Carrying her most of the way, they stopped at two more houses.

The tired little fairy turned from Mary Grant's door, handed her candy to her mother and then raised her arms for Anson to pick her up. "I tired."

Emotions played across his face before settling into a tender smile. He scooped her up and cradled her against his chest. "I think you have a ton of candy, little one. Are you going to share with me?"

Her ponytail bounced as she nodded. "Share nice."

Tess's chest tightened. The sweet moment both terrified and pleased her, causing an emotional civil war inside her head. The temptation to let him in was strong, but… The danger. She stepped closer to the two of them and rubbed her baby's back between the set of shimmery wings. "Let's get you home, sweetheart."

"Is she okay?" Anson whispered over the top of Hannah's head.

"When she gets excited, she wears out easily." She started toward home and couldn't bring herself to go into any detail about Hannah's heart condition or the surgery looming in the near future. Not tonight. Not when they were having such a nice evening.

They made their way through the thinning crowd, each of them lost in their own headspace. That didn't keep Tess from noticing the curious—and occasionally jealous—looks they received from passersby. She was pretty sure she'd identified several disgruntled members of his "Pantie Posse." Embarrassment mixed with an unexpected urge to boast about being the woman beside him.

"She's already asleep," he said, and waited for Tess to go up the front steps of her house ahead of him.

"I'm not a bit surprised." As they stepped inside, he was close enough for her to feel the warmth of her sleeping child, her sweet lollipop scent mixing with his spicier musk.

Anson shifted Hannah into a cradled position, one fairy wing poking out from under his arm. "I had fun tonight."

His voice was a husky whisper that zinged straight to her core. "Me, too." She put the candy-filled pumpkin on the coffee table and took in the sight of her child cuddled so tenderly in a man's arms.

Is it possible? Can I risk my heart—our hearts?

"Tess, can we be friends again?"

Friends? A stone dropped into her gut. Maybe it was the magic of Halloween and his flirtation, but for an irresponsible moment she'd let herself slip into a fantasy world where they might be more. "Yes… friends." She cleared the lump from her throat. "I better get her cleaned up and into bed. Thank you for going with us tonight. It meant a lot to my sweet girl."

"Thanks for letting me share it with you." He kissed Hannah's forehead.

When he moved closer and shifted the sleeping child into her arms, she resisted the urge to kiss his cheek. She needed a friend more than a temporary romance.

Anson turned the dead bolt and stood in the foyer staring into the mirror beside the coatrack, his image veiled dreamlike and hazy in the old silvered glass. The slight weight of the small child he'd held in his arms and the alluring scent of the woman were forefront in his mind.

"Anson? Something wrong? Anson?"

Nan's voice pulled him from jumbled thoughts. He shook his head and turned to her. "Sorry. What did you ask me?"

"Is everything all right? You look worried."

He didn't want to admit that the safety of his heart was in question. "I'm just concerned about going out of town tomorrow."

"I hope none of your concern is about me. I'm perfectly capable of taking care of myself for a weekend." To prove her point, she stepped away from her walker. "Come into the kitchen and have a cup of hot chocolate."

He thought better of arguing or scolding about her walker, and instead took her arm as they headed into the kitchen. "I'm happy to see how much better you're getting around, but I hope you're still okay with Jenny staying here while I'm gone."

"Yes—don't get yourself in a twist. How was trick-or-treating?" She let go of his arm and moved to the stove, where a pan of chocolate simmered.

He smiled, recalling the little one's excitement. "Hannah had a really good time and wore herself out. I carried her home, and she was sound asleep before we got there." Anson took one of the mugs she'd filled and sat at the breakfast table.

"Tess is a very mature, strong-willed young lady." Nan settled into her own seat. "Do you know how old she is?"

"She'll be thirty-two in November. Her birth date was on the lease agreement."

"She looks twenty-five and acts forty."

He chuckled but couldn't disagree. "I imagine being the single mother of a special needs child has something to do with that."

Her thin fingers wrapped around the blue mug, and she stared into her drink. "I think it's more than that."

"She's experienced a lot of loss, and I think she had to grow up fast. Her mother, father and brother all died by the time she was nineteen. I can't imagine what that would be like. Granddad is the only close relative I've lost."

"Poor dear," Nan said. "She's doing a beautiful job with Hannah, but they need more support in their lives."

"You're right."

"She initially comes off very serious, but there's a lot of sweetness underneath."

And passion. He ducked his head, just in case his feelings showed on his face. After tonight, Anson had no doubt of her capacity for empathy. She'd recognized the sadness in a little boy's eyes and forgiven him even when his teeth marks still showed on her daughter's skin.

"You look tired, dear. Go get some sleep before your trip tomorrow." She stood and kissed the crown of his head.

"Thanks for the hot chocolate." Anson's thoughts drifted back to his grandmother's statement about Tess needing support. He didn't know much about Hannah's father—other than him being a pathetic excuse for a man—but he'd been on alert since Tess's strong reaction to the mention of him.

Did he abuse her? Was she running from him?

Chapter Seven

When the carpenters repairing the museum's tin ceiling began putting away their tools and discussing Friday happy hour, Tess decided she'd also accomplished enough for the day. She'd sorted, researched and cataloged two boxes of items and made Monday's To Do list. The weekend stretched ahead with possibilities, and she planned to take Hannah exploring. She winced at the realization she was disappointed Anson wouldn't be around this weekend to join in on an adventure, but she couldn't allow herself to get used to his company.

Once the carpenters had gone, she locked up and made her way across the square. Delicious scents wafted from the nearby bakery and restaurants. Her stomach growled, and she quickened her pace, debating the pros and cons of cooking versus collecting Hannah and coming back for a meal she didn't have to prepare.

She rounded the corner onto Eighteenth Street, and a gust of wind whipped past, tangling her hair across her face and obstructing her view, but carrying the sweet sound of her daughter's excited giggling.

Hannah sat on the bottom step of Nan's front porch with a huge, black dog curled up at her feet. "Momma, puppy."

"That's a mighty big puppy." Tess shared a smile with Nan and Jenny.

"It's the neighbor's dog, Clem," Jenny said. "He's always sneaking out of his yard, but he's a gentle giant." She rose from the porch swing and flipped her long ebony hair off her shoulder. "I'm going inside to check on dinner."

"Thank you, dear." Knitting needles clicked in Nan's hands. "How was your day at the museum?"

"Very productive." Tess sat beside her daughter, kissed the top of her head and received a thorough sniffing from Clem. "I think we're going to need more display shelves and cabinets."

"We should take a look in my attic. There's bound to be useful items stored up there."

Tess thrilled at the idea of exploring that playground of antiques and memorabilia. "Sounds great."

Hannah continued stroking Clem and telling him

about her favorite Disney movies. The dog rolled over, happy to listen as long as he received love.

"Anson called to tell me he arrived safely in Dallas," Nan said.

"That's good." Tess started to ask for details but didn't want to seem too eager. "He takes góod care of you."

"He had a good example. He's just like his grandfather. Isaac was a jewel of a man, and we were very lucky to have him in our lives for so many years."

An ache prodded the empty places in Tess's heart. "Very lucky. Family is…precious."

"So true."

"Puppy play," Hannah said, and led the dog into the yard.

"Anson asked about you and Hannah when we spoke on the phone earlier."

"That was nice of him." She busied herself watching Hannah and feigning indifference. Nan's chuckle told her she hadn't done a believable job.

"I've lived a lot of years, young lady. I know when two people share mutual attraction."

Tess ducked her head. No need to display her tell-all expression and give Nan more matchmaking fuel. "You're not talking about me, are you?"

"I most certainly am. What's holding you back?"

"From what?"

"Admitting to yourself that you have feelings for my grandson."

The warmth of a blush spread from her chest to her face. "It's not like that. I hardly know him."

"Took me one afternoon to fall in love with Isaac, but I didn't let him know right away."

"We're only in town for a short time. And from what I've seen, he has no lack of women eager to date him."

The older woman dismissed Tess's statement with a flip of her hand. "None who catch his eye as you do."

Tess shook her head, as much for herself as for Nan. "He only wants to be friends. He said so."

"Sometimes young folks don't know what's good for them."

It was Tess's turn to chuckle. "We're both in our thirties."

Nan ignored that bit of information and continued. "You and my stubborn grandson are good for one another. It's that ex-husband of yours, isn't it?"

There was no reason to lie to this observant lady. "He has a lot to do with it."

"What did the rat bastard do?"

Tess snorted a humorless laugh. "That's an excellent description of Brent. He divorced me before Hannah was born. After we discovered she would have Down syndrome."

Nan's fingers drummed on the arm of her wicker chair. "He left you all alone?"

"Yes, ma'am."

"You remind me of Anson. The way he holds himself back from relationships and the opportunity for love. He has a lot to give and is going to make a wonderful husband and father. If only he'd open his heart again."

That got Tess's attention. "Again? What happened?"

"When he was getting out of the Marines, he eloped and came home with a wife. I knew from the moment I met her that she'd be trouble."

A pinched expression deepened Nan's wrinkles and told Tess what she thought about the woman her grandson had brought home. "I take it you were right?"

"She made his life miserable more often than not. Mine, too. I know about bad first marriages. I also know how wonderful it can be when you get it right. My second marriage was the best decision of my life."

Jenny stuck her head out the front door. "Supper is ready."

Tess stood. "Thank you both so much for looking after Hannah today. I think we'll head back to the diner for our supper."

"Nonsense," Nan said. "You'll stay and eat with us."

"I cooked enough for everyone," Jenny added with a smile.

"In that case, we'd love to." She might have to hear more well-meaning encouragement about her nonexistent love life, but she enjoyed their company, and so did Hannah.

* * *

Monday morning, Tess startled awake. The crying was real, not part of the bad dream in which her daughter fussed about moving to Houston. In her rush to get out of bed, the blanket tangled around her leg and she caught herself with one arm as she fell to the floor.

"Ouch. I'm coming, sweetie."

One touch to Hannah's damp forehead revealed her fear. Fever.

No! Damn it. I knew that lollipop would come back to haunt us.

She ran through the list of why this was horrible timing. Upcoming heart surgery, getting Nan sick, her job. But illness didn't care and never chose an appropriate time to rear its inconvenient head.

She cuddled her sick child. "I'm so sorry you feel bad. Tell Momma what hurts."

"Owie." Hannah touched her throat.

"Does it hurt when you swallow?"

Her answer was a nod with a tear sliding down her red cheek.

She carried Hannah to her bed and settled her under the covers. Hannah whimpered and she grabbed her cell phone, pulled up her contacts and hit Anson's number. As it rang, it occurred to her that she'd called him without giving it a second thought.

"Tess, are you okay?" he said after three rings.

That's when she noticed it was barely past five o'clock in the morning. "Oh God. I just realized what time it is. I'm sorry I woke you. I know you got in late last night."

"It's fine. What's wrong? I can hear it in your voice."

"Hannah is sick. Do you know if there's a good pediatrician in town?"

"Yes. Dr. Clark. What's the matter with her?"

"Fever and a sore throat. I knew that germy lollipop would come back to bite us in the butt."

"Let me make a call and see if I can get him to come over."

"To the house? Like a house call?"

"You're not in the big city anymore. I'll call you back in a few."

The line went dead and she stared at the phone in her hand.

"Momma, owie."

"Let me go get something to make you feel better, sweet girl." With a practiced hand, she measured out a dose of liquid pain reliever. "Open your mouth and take the orange medicine, please."

More used to taking medicine than any child should be, Hannah popped open her mouth, but whimpered when she swallowed.

Tess settled Hannah on her lap in the rocking chair that had belonged to her great-grandmother. Anxious about missing Anson's call, she checked her phone for the tenth time, just to make sure the ringer was on. It buzzed in her hand with a text message.

Help is on the way.

Fifteen minutes later her doorbell rang, and she opened it for Anson and a tall, gray-haired man with an honest to God old-fashioned doctor's bag in one hand.

"Good morning. I'm Dr. Timothy Clark."

She shook his extended hand. "I'm Tess Harper."

"Pleasure to meet you, young lady. I hear we have a sick little one."

"I'm afraid so." She ushered them inside and returned Anson's smile, ignoring the flutters his presence always triggered. "Thank you so much for coming, Dr. Clark." Suddenly aware of her disheveled appearance, she tightened the belt on her robe and attempted to smooth her hair. "This way, please. She's asleep in my bed."

The doctor followed, but Anson stayed near the front door.

Dr. Clark sat on the side of her bed and opened his leather bag. "Let's see what's got this baby feeling poorly."

"She's complaining of a sore throat and had a fever of one-hundred degrees. I gave her a dose of Tylenol."

"Sore throats have been making their rounds as of late."

She glanced over her shoulder to see if Anson had come into the room. With no sight or sounds from him, she assumed he'd left. Tess filled Dr. Clark in on Hannah's medical history.

"You've been lucky to hold off on surgery for this long."

"Yes, we have."

Dr. Clark pulled out his stethoscope. "Let's have a listen." He was extremely gentle and spoke soothing words as he woke Hannah, examined her and swabbed her throat. "I'll have the results of this culture back soon, but I'm going to start her on an antibiotic right away. Her little heart needs all the protection we can give it. Throw out her toothbrush. If my guess is correct, it's probably strep."

"Thank you so much for making a house call. Especially so early in the morning."

"I'm always happy to help new members of our community, and I only live a few blocks away. I'll call in the prescriptions. I'm going to put one on hold for you just in case you get sick, too." Timothy Clark clasped one of her hands between both of his. "Call me anytime day or night if Hannah needs me."

Several emotions flickered and threatened to embarrass her with tears. "Thank you. Let me walk you to the door."

"Remember to give her lots of fluids."

"I will."

"Good day." Dr. Clark waved to someone behind her, then crossed the porch.

She closed the door and turned, expecting to see that Hannah had gotten out of bed. Her pulse jumped at the sight of Anson leaning against her kitchen counter with one boot crossed over the other. "You were so quiet I thought you'd left."

"I wanted to make sure she's okay."

"Probably strep. It's going to be a rough couple of days, and I'll have to work from home." She reached for the bag of coffee beans, then realized the aroma of morning bliss already perfumed the air. "Hallelujah, sweet nectar. I could kiss you." *I can't believe I just said that!* She poured coffee and prayed her cheeks weren't turning three shades of crimson.

He did a poor job of hiding a grin behind the rim of his mug. "I figured you'd need it as much as I do. After getting home last night, I couldn't get to sleep."

"I definitely need a cup. Maybe two." After a large dash of cream, she savored her first sip. Had Anson been unable to sleep because he was thinking of her? She immediately scolded herself for the thought and pulled out baked goods. "Have a banana nut muffin with your coffee. Does the pharmacy have a drive-through? I need to pick up her antibiotic."

"No drive-through. I'll go get her medicine. You shouldn't take Hannah out in the cold."

She debated no more than a second before accepting his offer. "That would be great."

Anson bit into the homemade muffin and moaned. "Delicious," he said around a mouthful.

"Is Nan okay? We spent time with her this weekend and might've exposed her."

"She's fine so far. She was up and around when I left to come over here."

"Good. We can't have your grandmother getting sick." A slow smile brightened his eyes and made her stomach flutter.

"Other than her stroke, Nan hasn't been sick in years. I'll be back with Hannah's prescription as quick as I can."

"Is the pharmacy even open this early?"

"No, but the pharmacist lives right behind his shop. Plus, he owes me."

"Did you let him out of a speeding ticket?"

"Something like that." He wiggled his brows and took a step closer to Tess.

Her pulse jumped and she stiffened, thinking he was going to hug her—and wanting it more than not.

Instead, he picked up his mug for one last sip.

Her knuckles turned white as she tightened her grip on the edge of the counter. It was better that he hadn't touched her. He didn't need more sick germs spread across his body. And she definitely didn't need more fuel added to the fire of temptation.

After a successful trip to the pharmacy, Anson returned to Tess and Hannah with antibiotics, juice, Jell-O and a stuffed puppy. The soothing sound of Tess's voice drew him through the house to her bedroom. With her sick child cradled in her lap, she sang a song he'd never heard before.

"Hey there, little one. How are you feeling?"

Hannah blinked big sad eyes and didn't give him her usual smile. "Owie."

"That's what she calls being sick," Tess explained, and stroked her child's damp forehead.

Seeing her so miserable tore at his heart. "I'm sorry you're feeling bad." He pulled the toy out of the shopping bag and put it into Hannah's arms. "This puppy wants to keep you company while you get well."

"Tank you," she said, then whimpered and squeezed her new stuffy.

"Let's get this medicine into you, sweetie. Anson, do you know how to measure out the dosage that's listed on the front of the bottle? There should be a dropper or oral syringe with it."

"I do. I've helped my sister with my nephew, Landon." He put the shopping bag on the dresser, prepared the dose and handed it to Tess to administer.

"Open up, sweetie."

Hannah shook her head. "No!" Her flailing arm almost knocked the syringe out of her mother's hand.

Tess bit her lip, closed her eyes and inhaled deeply. "Hannah Lynn, you have to take this. It will help you feel better."

When Hannah cut a glance at Anson, he knelt to her level. "Do what your momma says, please. She's trying to make you better."

She looked back and forth between her mom and

Anson, then opened her mouth and swallowed the thick white liquid.

"That's my good girl. Have a sip of water, then I'll rock you to sleep."

He admired the woman who'd invaded his mind as she comforted her child with such tenderness. With no makeup and sexy bed head hair, she looked prettier than he'd ever seen her.

Wish I'd been the one to mess up her hair and... Damn.

He couldn't continue staring at her, so he grabbed the shopping bag and went into the kitchen to put away the items he'd bought. Before leaving for the pharmacy, he'd almost pulled Tess into his arms to comfort her, but she'd stiffened and something like panic had flashed in her eyes. Except for that one kiss in her moment of turmoil, she continued to keep him at arm's length. Could be when she was clearheaded she felt the same as him about short-term relationships. Maybe her attraction to him wasn't what he imagined it to be.

Certainly didn't help that I was a dumbass and embarrassed her when I told her to stop kissing me.

He'd been driving himself crazy with all the other things he should have said or done. Tess Harper was an irresistible woman who made him waver on his rule about not dating if it was only temporary, and he didn't know how much longer he could fight his desire.

Standing at the kitchen sink, he stared across the

yard at Nan's house and recalled his grandfather's stories of how long he'd chased her before she'd agreed to date him. The man hadn't given up and had been rewarded with a long, happy marriage.

Should I take the chance and try to thaw her icy shields?

Most likely, he'd be sorry, but in that moment, he decided he'd regret it even more if he didn't at least give it a shot.

Her leaving couldn't be as bad as what he'd already experienced.

Needing distance to think more clearly, he turned to go but couldn't leave until he made sure there wasn't something else they needed. He moved into the living room and once again studied the shelf of photos and memorabilia. Men in uniform, an old family photo of Tess as a child with her parents and brother at the beach and many pictures of Hannah filled the space. But none of Hannah with her absent father, or any other family member. Tess had lost everyone. They were alone.

The two framed flags caught his eye and something clicked. She'd lost her father and brother to violence in the line of duty.

Is my job the reason she pushes me away?

Tess came into the room and sagged into the recliner. "She's asleep again. I don't know what I would've done without your help this morning."

"I can see that was difficult for you to say." His tone was light and teasing.

She shot him a pointed glare that turned into a small smile. "You think you know me, Chief Curry?"

"You have to be observant in my line of work."

"Your line of work comes with a lot of dangers." She shivered and wrapped her arms around herself.

And my guess was correct. She worries about my job. "True, but not so much in a small town as in a big city."

She sat forward and adjusted her nightclothes. "What time do you have to be at work this morning?"

"I don't have to go in until noon."

"I hate to ask, but do you think you can stay long enough for me to get a quick shower? I don't want her to wake up and need me when I can't hear her."

"Sure. I can stay." He bit his tongue to keep himself from offering to wash her back.

Tess rushed through washing her hair but took a moment to let the hot spray beat against her upper back, right where tension gathered into a relentless knot. Right in that spot she couldn't reach to knead the soreness. It sure would be nice to have a strong pair of male hands working the kinks from her muscles. She chalked that fantasy up to a wishful daydream and turned off the water. She came out with wet hair, dressed in a pair of yoga pants and a tank top.

Anson's voice drifted from her bedroom. "Your momma is taking a shower, but she'll be out soon. Will you have another drink of water, please?"

Hannah sipped from the straw, then pushed it away. "No."

"How are you feeling, sweet girl?"

"No happy, Momma." She moaned, hugged her new stuffed animal and curled up on her side.

Tess smoothed the hair back from Hannah's forehead. "Try to go back to sleep while I walk Chief Curry out."

Anson rose from his seat on the bed. "Feel better, little one." He stretched as he walked slowly down the hallway.

His movements reminded her of a large cat on the prowl, but she was the one who wanted to pounce. "Shoot. I wasn't thinking when I asked you to stay. Now you have even more exposure to what's probably a contagious illness. Wash your hands and change your clothes before you handle anything Nan might touch."

"Yes, ma'am. Will do." He stopped with one hand on the front doorknob. "Call me if you need anything else."

Tess stood completely still, staring at the closed door for several moments before shaking herself out of a dreamy stupor.

Anson's good guy qualities and sexual magnetism were chipping away at her barriers—one tightly held piece at a time.

Anson did just as Tess requested and entered through the mudroom, threw his clothes in the washing machine and headed straight for the shower. When he was dressed in his uniform, he went to the kitchen for another cup of coffee. His mind was so focused on thoughts of Tess and Hannah that he startled when Nan cleared her throat.

"How's that sweet baby?" she asked from her seat at the kitchen table.

"She's definitely sick. Poor little one."

"I'll make a big pot of chicken soup and you can take it over this evening."

He sipped his black coffee and leaned against the center island. "Don't tire yourself out standing at the stove cooking all day. I know how long that soup takes to make."

She chuckled. "Aren't you the one who's been after me to get up and get back to the business of living?"

"Yes, but not all at once. Take it slow. Make sure Jenny helps you and use that walker that has the built-in seat on it just in case you need to sit in a hurry."

"If it will make you feel better." She stood and waved a hand to his right. "Take that sandwich and get yourself to work. Go make sure our little town is still safe to live in."

"Yes, ma'am." He grabbed his lunch and kissed her cheek. "See you after work, and I'll take the soup next door." It was a good excuse to see Tess again.

Damn, I'm like some infatuated teenager.

Chapter Eight

By the time evening rolled around, Hannah's fever had broken and she slept peacefully in Tess's bed. Exhausted and starting to feel sick as well, Tess headed for the kitchen to make a much-needed cup of hot tea. She added an extra dose of immune boosting tincture to hopefully prevent herself from full-blown illness. While the herbal brew steeped on the counter, she rummaged in the pantry for a can of soup to keep up her strength.

Someone knocked on her front door and she headed that way, but her head swam and she grabbed for the back of the recliner, knocking a plastic cup off the end table. Water splashed as the cup clattered across the floor.

"Tess, it's Anson."

"Give me a minute," she called out. "The floor is wet."

"Can I use my key?"

Light-headedness kept her rooted in place. "Yes. Come in." The lock clicked and the door swung open, but she remained clutching the back of the chair.

"I brought Hannah some of Nan's famous chicken soup." He closed the door with his foot, then paused and looked her up and down. "You're sick."

She held up a palm. "Stop. Don't get any closer. You shouldn't risk it again. I'm worried about you taking our germs back to your house. I'm just tired."

Anson ignored her, stepped around the puddle on his way to the kitchen and put a large, silver pot on the stovetop. "You need a bowl of this soup."

"I told you, I'm fine." She stepped in the water and threw her arms out to catch her balance. Her vision dimmed and she swayed, reaching for support again.

In a flash, Anson was beside her, clutching her against his chest. "You're not fine."

A quiver started in her belly and spread out along her limbs. She needed to step away and stop clinging to him. Stop inhaling his intoxicating scent. Independence warred with loneliness, and she gave in to the desire for a moment of comfort. "I know how to take care of myself."

"I have no doubt of that, but it's okay to ask for help now and then."

She sucked in a breath when he lifted her into

his arms, then laid her on the couch and sat at her feet. "Now look what you've gone and done. You've touched me and gotten completely germy."

He chuckled. "Germy?"

"You'll get sick." She attempted to sit up but eased back onto the cushions. "The second you get home, go straight to the shower and—"

"Tess." He squeezed her foot. "Are you admitting it?"

"What?"

"That you're sick."

Her throbbing head and scratchy throat could no longer be denied. "Yes, damn it all to hell and back. But I can't be sick right now." She covered her face to hide the threat of tears. His strong hands kneaded the muscles in her calves and made her want to crawl onto his lap and soak up a bit more comfort in his arms. "I have to take care of Hannah and work on the museum. I have to fight past this."

"You can also accept help. Lucky for you, my sister came to town this afternoon. She'll be there with Nan while I take care of you and Hannah."

"Like...stay here?" Her voice rose with each word.

"What? You're not going to let me sleep on my own couch?"

"Anson Curry, you can't be serious."

"Oh, but I am."

"I've taken care of Hannah and myself while both of us are sick. I can do it again."

"Well, this time you don't have to." He held up a

hand. "I know. You don't need help. But you said it yourself—you can't send me home all germy to get Nan sick."

She tried to find a reasonable argument, but only sighed and pressed her fingers to her throbbing forehead. "I guess you can stay. But only to protect Nan."

He clenched his jaw, but the hint of a smile pulled at one corner of his lips. "Will you eat a bowl of chicken soup?"

"That actually sounds wonderful. It's homemade?"

"It is. Nan is famous for making this soup. Even Dr. Clark swears by it." He pulled her up to stand and cradled her against his body. "Be still for a minute, in case you're dizzy again."

Her cheek rested on the slope of his pec, and she didn't have the strength or desire to question his motives, especially when his fingers worked magic on the tension in her back.

"I'm not being a very good nurse. I should probably let you stay on the couch and bring the soup to you."

Even feeling horrible, she smiled against his shirt and couldn't resist a bit of playful banter. "You just wanted to cop a feel, didn't you?" His deep chuckle vibrated against her cheek.

"Busted. Lie down and get comfy."

She had a perfect view of him preparing their meal, then putting it on TV trays he pulled out from under the couch. This was the first time a man had ever fussed over her like this, and it brought a sting to the back of her eyes as she once again fought the tears she was determined not to shed.

The room was quiet, except for the scraping of spoons against china, and the silence rattled her nerves. "Who's Brenda Curry?"

He jerked, and the spoon fell from his hand and clattered on the floor. "My ex-wife." His words were almost a growl.

"Oh. Sorry I brought it up."

"How'd you know her name?"

The prescription she'd discovered had been hidden, but her brain was too tired to think of an excuse. "I found something with her name on it."

"What was it?" His gaze scanned the room like the answer would jump out of hiding.

Damn. I should've known a cop wouldn't let it go at that. "An old prescription."

"I rifled this whole house to rid it of any trace of her." He retrieved his spoon from the floor and crossed to the kitchen. "Where did you find it?"

"If we were playing the Hot or Cold game, you'd be burning up."

His head cocked to the side as one brow lifted. "What game?"

"That one where you're looking for something and someone tells you if you're close by saying hot or cold. The prescription was taped on the underside of that drawer you're touching."

He jerked his hand away like it really would scald him. "Seriously? Where is it now?"

"In that red dish in the corner."

His jaw tightened as he studied the piece of paper. "Do you know what this is for?"

"Yes." The anxiety on his face had her concerned, and she feared telling him, but he'd find out eventually. "Birth control pills."

He tossed it on the counter and scrubbed his hands over his face. "I don't know why I'm surprised. I shouldn't be."

"I'm a good listener if you want to tell me about it. Grab a clean spoon and come sit down before your soup gets cold."

"Got any beer?"

"No. Sorry. I have wine and half a bottle of dark rum."

"Mind if I have some of the rum?"

"Help yourself. It's in the cabinet above the stove."

He pulled it out, poured a shot into a tumbler and rejoined her on the couch. "I shouldn't bother you with this. You need to rest."

"I'm still eating. And I could use the distraction." She scooped up another bite of Nan's delicious chicken soup.

Anson swirled the golden-brown liquor then took a gulp. "We got married because she was pregnant. Shortly after the wedding, she claimed to have a miscarriage."

"Claimed? You think she tricked you?"

"I suspect so. She acted like she was anxious to try again. When she wasn't getting pregnant, I started pushing for us to see a fertility specialist. We had moved to Oak Hollow by then. She kept putting it off, then one day announced she was pregnant. And once again had, or pretended to have, a miscarriage." He gulped down the rest of the rum in one shot, then plunked the glass down onto the tray.

"What made you suspect she was faking?"

His shoulders rose, then fell as he gave a deep sigh. "Lots of little things didn't add up, and both times it happened when I was conveniently out of town."

"Can't a doctor tell those kinds of things?"

"The first time she went to a doctor who happened to be one of her friends. A friend I never trusted. The second time was here in town. When I got home, I insisted she go to the hospital, but she refused. We ended up having a huge fight. She said she'd already been through it and was familiar enough with the signs and there was no need."

"That must have been a difficult time." She placed her spoon in the empty bowl and leaned back on the couch. "Why do you think she did it?"

"She knew how much I wanted to have a family and thought it was a good way to get her hands on the money she thought I had. And the money she assumed I'd inherit after seeing photos of Nan's house. She went on and on about how much she wanted lots of children but turns out she had no intentions of ever having any." His knee rapidly bounced, rattling his TV tray. "You know one of the things that haunts me most? I've never been sure if she wasn't actually pregnant the first time. I've always wondered if she had an…" He swallowed hard and shook his head.

A sympathetic ache tightened her chest, and she had a pretty good idea what he'd stopped himself from saying. "You don't have to say any more. I know how it feels to be duped by a spouse. My ex-husband made all kinds of promises about how things would be."

"Did he keep any of them?"

"Only one. The family house where we lived in Boston was a fabulous old colonial."

His gaze found hers and a look of camaraderie passed between them. "Brenda never liked this house. Once she moved out, which she did rather quickly, I found a hidden pack of birth control pills. The prescription you found makes sense." Disgust crumpled the skin around his eyes and curled one corner of his top lip. "The date on that script is right around the time I found out the truth. Guess she didn't have time to get a refill before I discovered her deceit."

"Have you seen her since then?"

"Nope. Have you seen your ex?"

"No. I didn't even see him when I signed the quickie divorce papers their connections secured. His mother practically presented them to me on a silver platter and requested my signature in blood."

Her remaining strength was fading fast, and she sank deeper into the cushions with a sigh. She tensed when he clasped her hand that lay on the cushion between them.

"That's harsh." Anson pulled her hand to his cheek, then pressed his lips to her palm. "Your hand is really hot. I think you have a fever."

A shiver shook her whole body. The heat that spread up her arm was not from any fever. "Is that how you take temperature?" *Because I like it. A lot.*

"It's one way. Not sure how accurate it is, though." He squeezed her fingers once more, then let go.

"Guess I better get some rest. Thank you for bringing soup. Hannah will like it, too."

"I'll give her some if she wakes while you're asleep. Back to the topic of meds, I think I need to go fill that just-in-case script for the antibiotic Doc sent in for you."

"You're probably right."

"Wow. A woman telling me I'm right. I better note the date and time." He grinned and got to his feet. "I'll go get it now."

"You're really racking up the good deed points, and I'm going to owe you big-time."

"We can work out the details of your repayment at a later date." He put a hand on the small of her back and guided her toward her bedroom, where Hannah slept.

She pulled back the covers and slid in beside her sleeping daughter. When he turned to go, she grabbed his hand. "Anson…" Emotion clogged her throat and cut off her whispered attempt at a thank-you.

He nodded, seeming to know what she was trying to tell him. "Be back soon." He slipped quietly from the room, and the front door closed a moment later.

She tucked one arm around Hannah and thanked all the stars above that Anson was here and willing to help her, even after the way she'd acted toward him on several occasions. She closed her eyes and tried to rest.

The next thing she knew, Anson was waking her to take an antibiotic capsule.

"Go back to sleep, honey," his deep voice whispered. "I'll be on the couch if you need me."

With an unusual sense of comfort, she allowed herself to close her eyes and drift back into dreams.

Anson startled awake and his eyes popped open. The room was still dark, but someone was patting his cheek. He snapped into awareness, sat up and swung his legs off the couch. "Hey, little one. What are you doing out of bed?"

"I thirsty," Hannah said.

"Let's get you something to drink." He picked her up as he stood. "Is your momma still sleeping?"

"Momma owie," Hannah whispered, and held a finger to her lips.

"I know. You look like you're feeling a little bit better." He pressed his cheek to her forehead and could still detect a low-grade fever. "Let's get you a sippy cup of juice."

He attempted to make it with her still on his hip but gave up and seated her at the table. He also checked Tess's handwritten list of when she'd given Hannah any medicine, then measured out a dose of fever reducer.

Hannah took the medicine without argument and downed half the cup of apple juice before pulling it from her mouth and sighing.

"You really were thirsty. Will you eat some chicken soup? Nan made it."

"My Nan soup?"

Her words strummed several chords in his heart. He'd gladly share his grandmother with this special little girl. "That's right. She made it just for you." He filled a small bowl and put it in the microwave. After he'd encouraged her to eat almost the whole bowl, he experienced her resistance to teeth brushing. "Are you ready to go back to bed, little one?"

"Rock chair, pease."

It took him a moment to translate her words. "You want me to rock you?"

She nodded and held her arms out to be picked up.

He scooped her up, then took her into her mother's room, where the chair sat beside Tess's bed. As quietly as possible he settled into the chair and began to rock. Hannah tucked both of her hands under her chin and curled herself against his chest. He held her a little tighter and began to sing a song he remembered Nan and his mother singing to him once upon a time.

His gaze drifted from the little one in his arms to the woman in the bed. Tess's hair was draped across her pillow in a spray of silky darkness, and he ached to feel its softness trailing through his fingers.

Oh boy. I'm in deep, now.

Tess woke to a deep male voice singing a lullaby. The sound wrapped around her, and a dreamlike fog clouded her head. She thought she was having a strange fever dream, but it was a good one. She snuggled deeper into the blankets in hopes of continuing the lovely hallucination, until the sound of Hannah's cough had her eyes popping open. She blinked, trying to adjust to the darkness.

Anson was sitting in her grandmother's rocking chair with Hannah cradled in his arms, smiling up at him like he was the best thing in the world. Tess held her breath, not wanting to interrupt the moment and wanting to see what would happen next. Her heart ached and filled at the same time. This big strong man was as tender as a lamb with Hannah. He accepted her without letting her differences get in the way. He treated her like any other child. Hell, he treated her better than her father.

People didn't always do that for her baby girl. It tore at her heart when people behaved awkwardly around Hannah, not knowing what to say or do or how to treat her. Others just ignored her. Few were as immediately accepting as Anson and Nan.

Anson moved seamlessly into another song. Hannah's eyes closed and her breathing evened out to her normal sleep pattern. Tess couldn't take her eyes off them. It was a scene she had longed to see since the moment Hannah was born.

I should be jealous of their connection or mad at him for pushing his way into our world...but I'm not. I'm sad and angry that my sweet baby girl doesn't have a father like him in her life every day. Can I risk letting him into our lives?

Her breath shuddered as emotions swelled in her chest.

Anson glanced up and stopped singing. He swallowed hard and his brow rose.

She smiled, trying to convey feeling she couldn't put into words. He released a breath he must have been holding and the corners of his mouth turned up, this time just for her. It was the kind of smile he'd given her on the day they'd met. Better actually because it was more tender and held meaning she couldn't quite name, but something was there. Something she wanted to explore. A flutter erupted in her chest, and she wasn't sure if it was anticipation or panic. Tess propped herself up on one elbow as he stood and nestled Hannah back onto the bed beside her.

"Sorry I woke you. I'll let you get back to sleep." He rounded her bed and left the room.

All she wanted to do was follow and let him hold her the same way he'd held her daughter. It had been far too long since she'd felt the touch of another human other than her child. It was the middle of the night, but she tucked the blankets around Hannah, climbed out of bed and went into the bathroom for Tylenol PM.

"God in heaven. I look horrible. Good thing I'm not trying to impress anyone." *Liar!*

She swallowed two pills and did the best she could with a hairbrush. When she stepped into the living room, Anson was stretched out on the couch with both arms tucked behind his head. She would not ask him to hold her, but she could at least have someone to talk to until the pain reliever kicked in.

He sat up when he saw her. "Sorry I woke you. How are you feeling?"

She cleared her throat and winced at the pain. "I'm hoping a cup of hot medicinal tea will help."

"Hannah came in here and woke me. I gave her some juice and she ate a bowl of soup. I also gave her Motrin and wrote it on your list. I was going to try to get her to fall back to sleep in here, but she said she wanted me to rock her."

Tess propped her elbows on the back of the recliner. "She likes to be rocked when she feels bad. Thank you for taking care of her. Want some tea?"

"I'll try some."

"I have to warn you about this particular tea.

Some people hate it. I add a syrup mixture I make myself."

His eyes widened. "What's in it? Eye of newt and bat tails?"

"Not in this batch," she said with all seriousness, but couldn't hold the expression and grinned. "Garlic, ginger, onion and turmeric soaked in apple cider vinegar, raw honey and cayenne pepper. After a few weeks, I strain it and then add it to herbal tea with more honey and lemon."

"Wow. That's quite a process. Sounds…"

"Weird?" she finished for him. "Can you handle spicy?"

He stood and stretched his back. "I love spicy food."

"Good. I'm going to make you try it." She motioned for him to follow her into the kitchen. "Especially since we're exposing you to our cooties."

He laughed, then covered his mouth and glanced toward the room where Hannah slept. "You always manage to surprise me."

They said little else and tap-danced around their attraction while she prepared the medicinal concoction. Once they were back on the couch, she sat at one end with him all the way at the other.

"Tell me about growing up in this small Texas town," Tess requested, then let a sip of warm tea slide soothingly down her throat.

"I loved it as a kid, thought I owned the town as a teen and then wanted out when I realized I didn't."

He sipped from his cup and grimaced. "Things didn't go as planned right after high school, so I joined the Marines. I saw enough of the world to make me realize I wanted to come back to Oak Hollow. So, here I am."

She wanted to ask what had gone wrong after high school, but something about the tone of his voice when he'd skimmed over the topic gave her pause. "That's the quickest life story I've ever heard."

"There are a few details I might've skipped over."

With her feet propped on the coffee table, she sipped her tea. "I've found that the middle of the night is the best time for considering those things that are too hard to think about during the light of day."

"It's also when the ghosts come out to play," he said.

"True. Sometime I'd like to hear more about your small-town childhood. I was mostly a city kid, and I've always wondered if my imagination has romanticized it into something more than it really is."

"We're all curious about the opposite of what we had."

"Before Hannah was born, I left Boston for Worcester. I had done some research and it was a good place for therapy and programs I thought she might need." And she'd wanted to get away from Brent's family. "Hannah has grown up in a city as well, but she really likes it here."

"What about you? How do you feel about my little part of the world?"

"I like it, too. I…" A yawn interrupted her speech, and she put her half-finished mug of tea on the coffee table.

"You can barely keep your eyes open. You should get back into bed."

"The meds I took had a sleep aid in them, and I think they're working." She stood and held out a hand palm forward when he made to rise. "I'm okay. Good night, Anson."

If he touched her again, she wasn't sure if she could control herself and not ask him to hold her all night long.

The next morning, Tess tiptoed into the living room and watched Anson sleep on a couch that was much too small for him. His bare feet stuck out from under the blanket and hung off the end. Why hadn't she thought to tell him to sleep in Hannah's bed? As she got closer, she could see sweat beading across his forehead. Very carefully she placed her palm on his moist skin. Fever.

As she'd feared, Anson had joined their sick society. Her gaze moved along his jaw to the muscles of his shoulders and the blue T-shirt molded to the dips and planes of his chest. It took her a moment to realize his eyes were open and staring at her.

"I don't think your tea worked," he grumbled. "I feel like hell."

"I was afraid of this. I did warn you, but I'm still sorry. I'm going to give you one of my antibiotic pills until we can get some for you. And I want you to go get into my bed. This couch is too small for you."

A half grin appeared, and he pushed himself up to sit. "You wait until I'm sick, *then* you ask me to your bed?"

"Very funny, wise guy. I already gave Hannah a bath and she's watching a movie in my room. You can go to her bedroom and sleep in peace or watch the movie with her in mine. I'd like to take a shower."

"What? I don't get an invitation to the shower, too?"

His words made her stumble, and for a moment, she considered asking him to come wash her back. And maybe a few other sensitive areas on her body.

After her lonely shower, she found Anson and Hannah watching a Disney movie in her room. She climbed onto one side of the bed with Hannah between them. "Are there any restaurants that deliver? We'll soon run out of soup, and I still don't feel well enough to cook. Just taking a shower sapped all my energy."

"We don't need takeout. I talked to Nan. She and some of the other ladies have been cooking, and Jenny will be over in a few minutes with loads of food."

The doorbell rang and Hannah imitated the sound. "Ding dong, Momma."

"I think I love this town," Tess said.

"Told you that you would." Anson winked and headed for the door.

After they'd eaten, they all three climbed back into bed to watch another movie. Halfway through, Tess realized Hannah and Anson were sound asleep. Light from the TV flickered across his face, and she took the opportunity to stare at him. His features were ruggedly handsome and all male, but relaxed in slumber she could see the gentleness she sensed within him. She'd been planning to set Anson up in Hannah's room for the night, but he looked so peaceful she couldn't bring herself to wake him. She turned off the movie and quickly followed the two of them into dreamland.

Tess woke in the night, as she normally did to check Hannah. Her child slept soundly, curled up between her and a man who had found his way into their lives. And their hearts. She reached across the space between them and touched his arm. He moaned, grimaced and mumbled in his sleep.

She recalled friends complaining about their husbands being big babies when ill. Funny terms like him-fluenza and dude-onic plague came to mind. She stifled a laugh, stroked his forehead and ran her fingers through his short blond hair.

He sighed, and one corner of his mouth twitched up. *I could get used to this. And that terrifies me.*

* * *

The next time she woke it was morning and Hannah was patting her face. "I play toys, Momma."

She pulled her into a hug and pressed her lips to her cheeks and forehead. No fever. "I'm glad you're feeling better. Are you hungry?"

"No yet." Hannah climbed over her mother and ran into her bedroom.

The sweet sound of her singing to her stuffed animals drifted down the hallway.

A deep male groan came from her unlikely sickbed partner, and she rolled to face Anson.

"I feel like hammered hell on horseback."

She chuckled. "Ouch. Laughing hurts my throat."

"I feel even worse for the little one if she felt half this bad."

Tess sat up and wrapped both arms around her knees to stretch out the knot of tension in her upper back. "I've heard whispered rumors about grown men feeling worse than small children. Or maybe it's grown men turning into small children when they're sick."

"At the moment, I can't argue with that logic."

"I bet you're regretting helping us about now," she said, while reaching back with one hand to try and press on the knot of muscle in that unreachable spot.

"Never. And I've never had such a pretty nurse. Turn your back to me and let me work on it."

She scooted close, sat cross-legged and presented her back. "I've got a kink right in the upper center."

She gasped when he pressed his fingers against the knotted muscles. It was quickly followed by a sigh when his strong hands slipped under the back of her T-shirt and worked magic on her tension. "That feels sooo good. Yes, right there. Harder."

His hands splayed and stilled on the bare skin of her back. "Damn, honey. Are you torturing me on purpose?"

"What?" She glanced over her shoulder to see his eyes blazing and his breathing heavy. She replayed the last few seconds and pressed her teeth into her lower lip to contain her smile. "You can stop rubbing my back if it's too taxing for you while sick."

"Not in the way you're thinking."

Despite her resistance, he'd tapped into a part of her she'd closed off since her marriage to Brent, and she didn't want to give up the missed playfulness. "Since we're both sick, maybe we should just stay in bed and moan together all day."

His bark of laughter was quickly cut off by a hiss. "You're right. Laughing hurts my throat, too."

Tess lay on her side facing him. "I better force myself out of bed and get Hannah to eat something. Us, too."

"You're a really good mother."

For some reason, his compliment almost brought tears to her eyes. Then suddenly, she knew why. Every second of every day she worked to be the best mother she could. A mother Hannah deserved. But sometimes the weight of doing it all alone left her weary. And so lonely for adult companionship. "I try my best. Every day."

"I can see that." He tucked hair behind her ear and trailed his finger along her neck.

The brief touch felt good. So good that one of the tears she'd been holding back slid from her eye. Just as she moved closer, ready to seek comfort in his arms, Hannah ran into the room and tossed an armload of stuffed animals onto the bed. A plush tiger and a blue bunny landed between them.

"Eat, pease." Hannah's plea swiftly ended what was almost their first cuddle session.

Intoxicated by the physical contact and connection they were forming, Tess was just brave enough to consider looking for another opportunity to… What?

What was she willing to let happen with Anson?

Chapter Nine

Anson couldn't take his eyes off Tess as she rolled from the bed, took her daughter's hand and glanced back with a mischievous grin before leaving the room. Fighting his attraction to her was becoming next to impossible. Especially with her loosening up and teasing him. He wasn't sure what hurt worse, the searing pain in his sore throat or the raging erection that would get no relief. Even sick, all he wanted to do was feel her warm soft skin sliding against his and…

"This line of thought isn't helping in the least," he mumbled.

"What's not helping?" Tess asked from the doorway.

"Lying here feeling sorry for myself." Thank God he was a quick thinker.

"Then get up and come eat with us. You need your strength."

Strength to resist you, little temptress.

He stopped in the bathroom and opened one of the six new toothbrushes he'd picked up at the pharmacy. When he entered the kitchen, Hannah was at the table eating oatmeal, and Tess was slumped against the counter waiting on something in the microwave.

Even sick and bleary-eyed, she was the most alluring woman he'd ever seen. He actually preferred her natural, with no makeup and her hair mussed and flowing around her shoulders.

"My chief sit." Hannah patted the table beside a glass of apple juice and a bottle of pain relievers.

"I'm glad to see you're feeling better, little one." He pulled out a chair, opened the bottle, shook out two tablets and winced as they fought their way down his flaming throat.

Tess slid a hot bowl of breakfast cereal in front of him, then went back for one of her own. "You better call Dr. Clark and tell him we've contaminated you."

"What we do?" Hannah asked her mother.

"We gave him our germs and he got sick."

Her lower lip poked out and she patted his hand. "I sorry."

He instantly felt a touch better. "It's okay, little one. Now I get to spend more time with you and your momma."

* * *

Anson had someone deliver his prescription and did his best to help take care of Hannah, but mostly marveled at Tess's strength and determination to soldier on through her agony. She rocked her child when she should've been sleeping, watched the same cartoon over and over, and cut food into special shapes. Keeping himself from gawking at this amazing woman was his biggest challenge, and the tension in his stomach was not from the illness. He might be thirty-five, but he felt like a teenager with his first crush, and he craved her like an addiction.

After a hot shower that night, Anson stood in the doorway of Tess's bedroom. Hannah stretched out like a starfish on the far side of the bed, taking up the middle and most of the area he'd been occupying. Her soft baby snores brought a smile to his lips, but the sight of her beautiful mother caused a completely different flutter deep in his chest. Looking especially tempting in a black tank top and shorts, Tess curled on her side facing her daughter. This time he didn't go around to the other side of Hannah. Anson slid in behind Tess and wrapped his arm around her waist. She held perfectly still in his embrace until he nuzzled his face in her shower-damp hair.

"You smell like apples," he said against her neck.

Her initial moment of surprise morphed into a shiver, and she tilted her head to give him better access. "It's my shampoo. You smell pretty good yourself, and your skin is so warm. Did you take your temperature?"

"No." He kissed the curve of her shoulder. "This heat is because of you." Her laugh vibrated against his chest, relieving his fear of her rejection.

"I think you give me too much credit." She laced her fingers with his as she pulled their joined hands against her heart. "I haven't been held like this in a really long time."

"It's been a while for me, too."

Tess shifted until they faced one another, their hands still linked between them. "For tonight…can we hold one another and…"

"And what?"

"I don't know." She pressed her forehead against his collarbone. "It feels good to be held by you. To hold you. I don't want to stop."

Stark need radiated from Tess and made his desire all the more powerful. He freed a hand and tilted her face up to meet his gaze. "You won't find me arguing. It's good to share human touch."

"But not just with anyone."

His thumb tingled as he traced the curve of her full lips, and he recognized the caution and fear in her eyes. "You're not just anyone."

"This sensation…this rush of excitement about a new connection is something you only get to experience once." Her voice quivered and a single tear slid from the corner of her eye.

He kissed the moisture from her cheek before she

had a chance to dash it away. "I know, and I'm right here with you."

"I want to enjoy this moment for what it is. And not…"

"Take things further?" he asked.

"Exactly. Not yet."

The pounding of his heart increased. *Not yet isn't a no.*

Tess slid her hand across his chest then into his hair at the nape of his neck. "Let's just savor this feeling for a little longer."

"You got it, honey." He couldn't deny wanting to carry her into another room, strip her bare and make love all night long. His body and mind were begging for more, but he also understood and would respect her wishes. This initial attraction only came along once, and he didn't want to rush past something that felt so good. So right.

But so scary.

After turning off the lamp, he wrapped his arms around her and settled her against his chest, wishing there were no barriers between his skin and hers. "We can stay in our own little bubble. All night."

She chuckled. "Good thing you feel that way, because Hannah is taking up the other side of the bed."

"I'm glad. There's nowhere else I'd rather be." He kissed her forehead, the tip of her nose, then took a few seconds to soak up her sweetness before slowly pressing his lips to hers. Her seductive moan sent blood surging through his body, but he fought it, determined to hold true to his promise.

She stroked his face with her fingertips and returned the gentle kiss before resting her head under his chin. "Sweet dreams, Anson."

There was so much tenderness, such a wealth of power in their connection. He felt a fierceness for this woman that he'd never known.

She stole his last bit of resistance. And his heart.

Tess woke to the first rays of dawn light filtering through the blinds. Hannah was nestled against her belly, and Anson spooned protectively behind her with his arm cradling her and her child. Waking up like this was a first for her and Hannah. A surge of intense sensations burst through her, and she wasn't sure if she wanted to laugh, break into happy tears, or cry for what they'd been missing for her daughter's whole life.

Together, they'd created a bubble of contentment that had carried them through the night. How could she freeze time and hold on to this moment forever? She closed her eyes and breathed in the baby powder scent of her precious child and the warm musk of the man behind her.

"I can hear you thinking," he whispered in her ear.

A wave of tingles followed the warmth of his breath, and she trailed her fingers along the muscles of his forearm. Perhaps he worried she'd push him away in the light of day, and she probably should.

But her daily ration of Nan's matchmaking added to a large helping of Anson's smooth ways had tempted her beyond resistance. For the first time since her divorce, she was willing to share something of herself with a man.

But not everything.

"I'm thinking…" She couldn't just blurt out that she'd like to wake up in his arms every morning… Until she left town. "This is a nice way to wake up."

"Should I get out of bed before Hannah gets up? I'm not sure what's appropriate in this situation."

A sudden tension filled her belly. "That's something I really should've considered before now. If we hadn't all been sick, this wouldn't have happened."

Hannah wiggled, tucked her knees under her tummy and poked her little bottom into the air.

"It's too late now," Tess said. "She's awake."

Hannah popped up like a jack-in-the-box. "Hi, Momma."

"Good morning, sweet girl." She smoothed the toddler's riotous curls. "How do you feel today?"

"No owie. My chief owie?" Her chubby fingers patted his arm.

"I'm feeling much better today. Your momma is a good nurse."

Hannah flung herself across the two of them, kissed each of their cheeks, then slid from the bed. "I play," she called over her shoulder and scampered from the room.

Tess rolled over to face him and nestled in the

crook of his arm. "It obviously doesn't bother her a bit that you're here."

"She did tell me it's nice to share. She's very accepting."

"If everyone had her sense of acceptance, it would be a beautiful world. She's usually a good judge of character, too." Tess splayed her hand on his chest and enjoyed the steady rhythm of his heart beating under her palm. Morning sunlight filtered through the blinds, casting slanted shadows. "These walls are really white. Have you ever thought about a color to warm up the room a bit?"

"Trust me. White is better than the awful pink that…they were."

Tess pushed up onto her elbow. "Oh my gosh. This is the bedroom you shared with your ex-wife. Is this totally weird for you?"

He sat up and leaned his back against the headboard. "You'd think so, but no. After Brenda left, I painted the walls and got rid of the modern chrome-and-glass furniture she insisted on putting in this room."

A growl threatened to rise in her throat, and she wrinkled her nose. "I know all about getting rid of things that remind you of an ex you'd like to forget."

"Momma," Hannah yelled from the other room. "Eat, pease."

"That's my cue. Time for breakfast and a round of antibiotics and gargling with salt water."

Anson climbed out of bed and pulled her to her feet. "How long before we aren't contagious?"

"We're already safe to be around. The rule is antibiotics for twenty-four hours and no fever. Are you eager to leave?"

"Not at all." He squeezed her shoulders as he followed her from the bedroom. "But I need to get back to work."

What she really wanted to ask is if their closeness would continue. And if they might share a bed again. Just the two of them, with the door locked.

Tess put away lunch leftovers and couldn't keep the smile from her face. The sweet sounds of Hannah singing along with a Disney sing-along mingled with the deep timbre of Anson's voice as he talked on his phone.

He walked into the kitchen and slid his phone into the back pocket of his jeans. "I need to go down to the station."

A surge of disappointment hit her, and she almost dropped the bowl she was putting into the refrigerator. Their brief isolation from the rest of the world was over. "I know I said you weren't contagious, but you really should get more rest before returning to work."

"I wish I could, but duty calls."

"What's going on? Is there trouble?"

"Tommy's father and one of his uncles got themselves arrested, again. Dealing pills. A bag of weed here and there is one thing, but hard drugs…" His lip curled on the last words. "Not in my town."

"Is Tommy okay? And his brother?"

"As far as I know, but CPS is involved, and I need to find out what's happening. I've got to go home and get my uniform." He pushed away from the counter and took a step but paused. "Thanks for taking care of me."

"I think we're even. You did a lot for us as well. Probably more."

His phone pinged with a text message and he pulled it from his pocket. "It's Walker. He wants me to go out to the Seaton place with him."

The dangers of his job resurfaced in a wave that slapped her in the face. "Better get to work, Chief." She rubbed the center of her chest where tension gathered.

"Tess." He gently cupped her shoulders, then enfolded her in an embrace.

For several moments, they held one another, and she found that perfect place to rest her cheek—right on the swell of his pec, tucked neatly under his chin.

"Would it be okay if I bring you and Hannah dinner later?" he asked.

She couldn't see his face, but heard uncertainty in his question and sensed that they shared a fear of rejection. "That would be nice. I could go for some of that pot roast you brought me on the night we arrived in town."

His arms loosened and they moved apart enough

to see one another. "Mac and cheese for the little one?"

"Of course. Don't push yourself too hard today." She still had a hold of his waist, and she wanted to kiss him, but ducked her head instead. His lips were warm and soft against her forehead before he stepped away.

She closed the front door behind him, braced herself against it and worked to calm her breathing. The swirling patterns on the old wooden floor gave her something to concentrate on, and for some reason made her think of dancing. And there was only one man she wanted to dance with.

"What the hell am I doing?"

The empty room wasn't offering up any wisdom, so she put one foot in front of the other and went to see why her child was being so quiet.

Hannah was curled up in the middle of her bed surrounded by a circle of stuffed animals and singing to Boo Bunny.

How amazing it would be to feel her daughter's level of serenity. As soon as she wished for a bit of that peace for herself, warmth filled her chest with the memory of a similar feeling. The flash of happiness and tranquility wasn't imagined or from a dream. Her moment of contentment in Anson's arms had been real.

And I deserved it.

Could she claim a bit more happiness for herself? Absolutely. But *should* she?

She and Hannah would be settled in Houston right after Christmas. A big city with plenty of job opportunities, great hospitals and doctors, and several great special needs school options. After Hannah recovered from heart surgery, they'd find the perfect neighborhood and house. Until then, she could enjoy her time in Oak Hollow, then move on to the next phase of their lives.

Anson knew she was leaving, so he wouldn't be expecting more than a part-time gig. Why not explore the possibilities and allow herself to be open to the idea of something temporary between them?

With a tentative plan where Anson was concerned, Tess left her daughter to her playing, pulled out her laptop and got back to work on the job she'd been hired for. There was plenty that could be accomplished on the computer, so going to the museum could wait one more day. Pushing herself too soon had been her downfall in the past, and her child needed her at full running speed.

Hannah entertained herself for another hour, had a snack and took a long nap, allowing Tess to get more than she'd thought accomplished. By late afternoon, they were both more than ready to get out of the house. Going far wasn't an option, so they went next door to see Nan and Jenny.

Hannah ran ahead of her mother and was about to open Nan's door.

"Hannah Lynn, stop. You have to knock. You can't just walk into someone's house."

"My Nan, Momma."

She knelt to her daughter's level. "Sweetie, I know you like her and she's your new friend, but you still have to knock, even at a friend's house. And since we've been sick, we can't hug her today."

The door opened and Jenny looked down at them. "I thought I heard voices."

"We're having a conversation about knocking and not just walking into someone's home."

"That's a good rule. You have to wait for someone to open the door before going inside."

"Door open," Hannah said, and then she darted past Jenny.

The two women shared a laugh.

"I need to check on something in the kitchen, but Nan is in the back sunroom. I'm sure Hannah has already found her."

Tess followed the path her precocious child had cut through the house and found her standing in front of Nan.

"Good afternoon," Tess said as she entered the cozy space.

"I'm so glad you two have come for a visit."

Hannah crossed the room to look at pots of violets on a windowsill.

"We were getting stir-crazy in the house, and I wanted to thank you for all the delicious home cooking you sent over."

"My pleasure. I'm glad to see you're both feeling better."

"Thanks in part to Anson's help."

"He seemed to be feeling pretty good when he came in to get ready for work. Whatever nursing you did sure put a big smile on my grandson's face." Delight was clear in Nan's laughing eyes.

"Nothing special. Just made sure he ate and took his medicine."

"You must have given it to him with a spoonful of sugar."

The other woman's innuendo brought a rush of heat to Tess's cheeks and a momentary loss of speech. Now would be a perfect time for Hannah to interrupt the conversation, but of course her child was on her best behavior at the moment. "I think Jenny said something about making tea. I'll go see if she needs help." She rushed from the room and found Jenny in the kitchen. "Is it all right if I make hot tea?"

"Sure. Nan didn't tell me she wanted any, but it'll go good with the shortbread cookies I just baked."

"She didn't ask for tea. I just needed an excuse to leave the room for a minute. Nan has a few ideas about what's been going on at my house over the last few days."

"That sounds like her. She has a reputation as a matchmaker."

"It seems I'm currently one of her reluctant clients."

Jenny chuckled. "I can confirm that's true. Could you hand me that oven mitt, please."

Tess passed it over and then filled the kettle with water. "Is she always trying to set Anson up?"

"She occasionally tries, but he's put his foot down a few times. I think she's been waiting for him to be ready before cranking up her efforts." Jenny pulled a tray of shortbread from the oven and the buttery scent of fresh baked cookies filled the room. "She hasn't stopped where I'm concerned, but I'm not complaining. Thanks to her, I have a date tonight."

"That's great."

"We're going to see a band play in San Antonio. I need to leave as soon as Anson gets here."

"If it's okay with Nan, I'll stay with her until he gets home."

"That would be great. She fusses about Anson believing she needs a babysitter, so I try to make it seem more like I'm here to help out around the house, not just watch her."

"I'll keep that in mind," Tess said, and put tea bags into the cups.

Tess and Nan relaxed on the back porch while Hannah sat beside one of the flower beds in the last glow of the fading sun.

The older woman picked up her needlework. "What's holding you back, dear?"

"From what?"

"Allowing yourself to love again."

I don't want to fall in love again! Trembling started in her belly and bloomed into a pounding in her chest. "I have to protect Hannah. If I get serious with a man, it could have a negative effect on her."

"It might lead to a happily-ever-after. We've discussed ex-husbands before, and I know that is a fear for you, but Hannah needs you to be happy so you can take care of her. You're young and beautiful. Someone to support and love you could be a wonderful thing for both of you."

"I…" Painful memories of her short marriage and quicker divorce assaulted her brain. And the first-hand knowledge that loved ones were often taken away too soon.

"Putting yourself back out there is a scary thing. I might be old, but I still remember. In my personal experience, the payoff can far outweigh the risk."

In Tess's experience, the pain of one loss on top of another could be crippling, and she worried about adding more sorrow and having it accumulate into something that might crush her. A huge gamble when Hannah was depending on her.

Nan set her needlework aside. "What's this job that's taking you to Houston?"

"Well… I don't actually have another job, yet. But I have a line on several options." Her gaze moved to Hannah meticulously laying out a row of pebbles along the top of a rock border.

"Then why are you moving there? Are the opportunities that great?"

She couldn't keep the truth from this woman any longer, and in all honesty, she needed someone to talk to. "We're going to Houston because Hannah needs open heart surgery."

Nan flinched, reached across the small side table between them and took Tess's hand. "Oh, my dear. I didn't know. Tell me about it."

"She was born with a heart condition, as many babies with Down syndrome are. We've actually been really lucky that we've been able to put it off this long. It's scheduled for January."

"And you'll be there all alone to go through it?"

Tess shrugged and stared at the thin, fragile hand in hers. She hadn't felt this kind of comforting maternal touch since her mother died years ago. "It's okay. I'm used to it."

"Pish posh. There will be none of that nonsense. Houston is not that far away, and I know just how to get there. We'll be there with you when the time comes."

"I couldn't ask—"

"You didn't ask. I offered, and I refuse to take no for an answer. Does Anson know about her surgery?"

"No."

"I'm going to give you some advice. You can take it or leave it, but I suggest you seriously consider it."

"Okay. I'm listening."

Nan squeezed her fingers once more, then reached for her glass of water and took a sip. "You can't go through the rest of your life so guarded or you'll end up bitter and unhappy. For your sake and your daughter's, let your heart be open to the possibility of love. You both need other people in your lives. And there are people right here in Oak Hollow that already adore both of you."

Blood rushed in her ears, and she sputtered incoherently before clamping her jaw. Everything Nan said made sense, and even though she was already considering a friends with benefits arrangement with Anson, that didn't mean she was comfortable putting her heart on the line.

She took a breath and prepared to voice her fears. "If I let Hannah get too attached, she'll be hurt if…" *If Anson decides he doesn't want us.* "She'll be hurt when we leave." *And so will I.*

Nan shook her head. "Oh, honey. You've seen Hannah and Anson together. That ship has sailed. They've bonded, and there's nothing you can do to change that."

Tess sighed with the truth of it. "She also adores you."

"And I her. I know it's hard, but you'll have to take the risk with your heart at some point."

Nan's advice swirled in her head. Enjoying the time they had in Oak Hollow was one thing, but planning anything beyond that with Anson was ill-advised.

A gray-and-white cat Tess had never seen slowly crept out from under a cluster of vines and headed tentatively toward her daughter.

Hannah rolled onto her belly and propped her chin on her hands. "Hi, kitty cat."

The animal stopped a foot away and settled on its belly with his front paws crossed.

Hannah continued talking to the wary cat as it inched closer and finally sniffed her extended fingers.

"Nan, is that your cat?"

The other woman glanced up from her needlepoint. "Would you look at that. We feed him, but he's just a stray with a fondness for my yard. He's never let anyone touch him before."

Tess stood and walked to the edge of the porch. "Should I shoo him away?"

"They seem to be getting along okay, but I'd hate for him to scratch her."

Not wanting to startle the skittish cat, she slowly descended the limestone steps.

The stray glanced her way, backed away from Hannah, then darted through the flower beds and around the side of the vintage glass greenhouse.

"Momma," Hannah scolded, "you scare kitty cat."

"Sorry, sweetie. I didn't want him to hurt you."

"No hurt." She held her hands up as proof. "Nice kitty cat."

The screen door squeaked, then slammed, and Anson crossed the porch. "Evening, ladies."

Tess's insides trembled at the sight of him.

"Hello, dear," Nan greeted. "Guess who made friends with your stray tomcat?"

He turned on a full watt smile, and Tess's pulse

fluttered in her throat. "You didn't tell me you had a cat."

He took the steps two at a time and crossed to them in a few strides. "He just started coming around. I call him Tom-Tom, and I've been working on making friends with him for months. Seems somebody else has the magic touch."

"I told you animals like her. She's like a mini Snow White."

When Hannah clung to his leg, he picked her up and tossed her into the air, eliciting squeals of delight before settling her on his hip. "Did you make a new friend?"

"Nice kitty cat. Where you puppy?"

"My puppy is still too little to come home. He's staying with my friend's momma dog until he's big enough."

Drawn by the heat of his body, Tess leaned against his shoulder.

"Down, pease." The little girl wiggled in his arms until he put her on her feet, then she ran toward Nan.

That's when Tess glanced over and met Nan's beaming smile. She ducked her head and lowered her voice. "Your grandmother is grinning at us like she's very pleased with herself."

Rather than stepping away, he wrapped an arm around her waist and pulled her closer. "She'll be full of herself, but this time, I don't mind. How'd you and Hannah feel today?"

Since their new closeness was no longer a secret,

she returned the embrace. And it felt surprisingly natural. "Not a hundred percent, but we needed to get out of the house. What about you?"

"I'll admit, I'm pretty beat. Dinner and rest sounds good. I picked up the food I promised from Acorn Cafe."

"What happened with Tommy's family?"

"He and his brother are staying with a great-aunt and-uncle while CPS finishes their investigation. They're an older couple, and the only decent adults in that family. Tommy's father and uncle couldn't make bail."

"What a mess."

"We should eat before the food gets cold." He turned them and headed toward the house.

"I hope it's okay that I sent Jenny home to get ready for her date?"

"Sure. I wondered why I didn't see her car."

"Do you want to…" The words *come over and hang out* caught in her throat.

"What?"

"Never mind." Hair tickled her cheeks with each shake of her head. "I'm sure you just want to go to bed after we eat."

His lips lowered to just a breath above her ear. "Depends on what bed you're suggesting."

She shivered and laughed simultaneously, his husky whisper stirring up butterflies in her belly. "I was going to ask if you wanted to watch a movie after Hannah goes to bed. One that isn't animated or about animals."

"I like that idea. Let's eat and get Hannah home for a bath."

Chapter Ten

Once Hannah's bedtime routine was accomplished, Tess and Anson tiptoed from her room and down the darkened hallway. Only the light of one lamp lit the living room, and the air sparked with sexual tension, making the fine hairs rise on her arms.

"I was surprised when Nan said she was going to get ready for bed right after dinner. Do you think she's feeling okay?" Tess asked.

"She's fine. She only went to bed because she wanted me to feel comfortable leaving her to come over here. Since she's suddenly able to get around with little trouble, I'm starting to suspect she's been physically stronger than we thought all along. I think she was staying in bed because she's having such a hard time after losing my grandfather."

Tess swallowed the lump that always appeared when she thought about the ones she'd lost. Her own mother had given up completely and allowed cancer to take her after the death of her husband and son. "Losing someone you love, especially someone you've spent a life with, like your grandparents, can wreck your will to live. I'm glad she's coming around." Tess crossed to the front door and checked the lock.

"Are you worried I'll escape?" Anson asked.

"Just habit from living in big cities." The intense gaze of his bedroom eyes sent a delicious shiver racing across her body. "I haven't locked the side door yet. Just in case you plan to make a run for it."

He dropped his large frame onto the middle of the couch and spread his arms across the back. "I'm happy right here."

Flutters filled her stomach. "Want a drink?"

"Not if it's garlic tea." His crooked grin lightened any sting his words might cause.

"Hey, that tea is probably why you got better as quickly as you did."

"True. I'll give you that."

She abandoned her safe spot by the front door but left the barrier of the coffee table between them, because what she really wanted to do was straddle his lap and kiss him senseless. "I can open a bottle of red wine."

"You get the wine, and I'll turn on some music."

"What about watching a movie?" she said, and considered diving across the coffee table when he leaned forward and a slow, sexy smile reached his eyes.

"I'd rather watch you."

Her heart leaped in her chest, desire radiating between them. "I… You…"

"Yes," he chuckled, and stood. "You and me."

"Wine. I'll get it." *Oh my God. I sound like a fool.*

She rushed into the kitchen, but it took her a moment to remember where she'd put the corkscrew and then she just stared at the bottle. Finally, she made it into the living room with two glasses of Malbec.

He stood beside the stereo with a thumb hooked in the front pocket of his jeans. "Dance with me?"

She took a bolstering sip, put the glasses on the coffee table and accepted his outstretched hand. The warmth of his palm calmed her nerves.

And heightened her desire.

Anson pulled her into a slow dance and sang along with Tracy Byrd's "Keeper of the Stars."

"This song is fitting. Hannah believes you *are* the keeper of the stars."

"I'll do my best to live up to her belief in me." He slid his fingers into her hair and tucked her head under his chin.

She'd thought keeping distance between them was the safest course, but the shelter of his arms felt like the most protected place in the world. The lyrics about fated meetings sparked closely guarded emotions, pulling her deeper into a dreamy fog. Was it possible the stars meant for them to be together? Did the universe have a plan? Destiny or random accident?

Just when she thought they couldn't get any closer, their bodies seemed to fuse, and they no longer moved around the room, only swayed as one. The taut corded muscles along his back flexed under her fingers, and the deep timbre of his singing vibrated against her breasts. Shivery tingles swept through her, and she gave up the last sliver of restraint and fell into their instinctual rhythm. The spicy musk of his skin, the heat of his touch and the solid press of his tall, broad frame all blended into a melody her body craved to hear.

"Sweet Tess," he whispered into her hair, then tilted her face up to meet his lips.

She recognized the fierce rush of need in his kiss, the stroke of his tongue sending flames licking across her skin. And a bonfire kindling in her core.

"Your skin is so soft." His mouth swept back and forth along her jaw.

With a tilt of her head, she gave him access to the curve of her neck. Hell, she was ready to grant him access to a lot more. "Anson, if you're going to tell me we need to stop, again, you better—" The teasing nip on her bottom lip halted her words... And thoughts.

"Please, don't ask me to leave...or stop."

She moaned as his low-pitched husky voice wrapped her in velvet heat. "Don't stop. Don't leave." With an urgency she couldn't ever remember feeling, she led him down the hallway.

Sheltered behind the locked door, he cupped her face. "Last chance to stop me before I make love to every inch of you."

In answer, she unbuttoned his shirt until it hung open, revealing a sun-bronzed chest with a small patch of blond hair between chiseled muscles.

His shirt fell to the floor as he unbuckled his belt and let it slide free from his jeans. "I've wanted you since the moment I first laid eyes on you, frantic as a hummingbird as you searched for your child. But now it's more than just lust for a stranger. I see you. I want to know you."

"What would you like to know?" She pressed her lips to his nipple and smiled when he moaned, fingers gripping her hips like he'd never let her go.

"I want to discover every secret place on your body, and which ones are the most sensitive." He gently kissed the curve of her shoulder before sliding his lips up her neck. "What sounds you make when I tease them."

When his teeth tugged her earlobe, she gasped and traced her fingertips over his quivering muscles and into the waistband of his jeans, loving the shuddering breath her touch elicited.

"I want to know your dreams…and secret desires."

"Let me show you." Tess pulled back enough to strip off her shirt and jeans, then flung herself against him. Her enthusiasm knocked them off-balance, and they fell onto the bed laughing.

"An eager lover is so sexy," he whispered, and unhooked her bra with one flick. "I want to feel you skin to skin. Taste you. Hear you gasping with need."

A response wasn't possible when he hooked his thumbs in her panties and slid them down her trembling thighs, an erotic fever rising under his touch.

Oh sweet mercy. I need this.

For years she'd missed the touch of a man, but their connection was beyond satisfying a biological need. And she was determined to enjoy every moment. Aching to explore him as he did her, Tess stroked his shoulders, thrilling at the power in the sculpted lines. His hot, wet mouth caressed her breasts, stopping to tease then moving lower, following the path of his hands. She'd swear he had a map of her body and a set of written directions, because his technique was magical.

I'm going to combust with pleasure.

Anson's head spun with need and pleasure. Her skin was like velvet. Her taste the sweetest candy. Her need matching his own. He filled his hands with her breasts, peaked nipples teasing his palms.

"Oh yes…" she sighed. "More."

He chuckled and kissed the trembling muscles of her stomach then the warm skin of her inner thigh, grasping her hips when she writhed and called out his name.

Tess tangled her fingers in his hair and tugged, but the twinge of pain only spurred him to further exploration.

She arched her back when he flicked his tongue against her, hands flung out on the bed. "Anson, please."

He made his way back up to her mouth, chest tight as unfamiliar emotions filled his head. And heart. "What do you need? What can I give you?" Her husky laugh hit him like a sledgehammer.

"You. I need you. Please," she moaned, breathy and slow.

Who was he to deny her such a sweet demand? His jeans and boxers hit the floor, but not before he retrieved a condom. Pressing his naked body against hers triggered an untapped spark. The start of a fire that branded him and burned so far beyond mere physical pleasure. Something that left him weak, yet his strongest ever. It was a sensation he'd remember forever. And it only got better when she wrapped her arms around him.

"Tess Harper, you rock my world."

"We're just getting started." She took his mouth, wild and demanding with a rawness that shook him.

He gave her all of himself, in a long, slow motion that brought them both to a feverish high. He caught and held her gaze, and for the first time he didn't feel the need to guard his expression. It had never been like this with any other woman.

They moved as one. Mingled gasps and shared moans. Hearts opening.

And protective walls coming down.

Her teeth pressed hard into the flesh of his shoulder before she tossed her head back, and her lips parted on the sexiest sound he'd ever heard. When she shattered around him, he followed with such force that his vision blurred, and he was surprised he'd remained conscious.

Anson rolled them onto their sides, but kept her in his arms, stroking her hair as he caught his breath. She clung to him, and he sensed her need for a bit of borrowed strength. "Rest, honey. I'm here."

Her lips brushed whisper soft against his. "I know you can't stay all night, but would you hold me until I fall asleep?"

"Absolutely." Her contented sigh brought a huge smile to his face. "Sweet dreams, honey."

Dare I dream of a future...with you?

Tess woke and stretched tender muscles, and a cat-that-kissed-the-cowboy smile spread across her face. Even with way less than her usual amount of sleep, she hopped out of bed, ready to start the day. Morning-after regrets were nonexistent, and she was anxious for an encore of their lovemaking. Too bad he couldn't have stayed the night.

Tess walked into her daughter's bedroom just as

she was sitting up. "Good morning, sweet girl. How did you sleep?"

"I dream. Puppies." Hannah raised her arms for morning cuddles.

"What a nice dream. Let's get dressed and eat breakfast. We're going on an adventure with Chief Anson today."

Hannah wiggled from the hug and rushed to her closet to pick out clothes.

When Anson rang their bell, Hannah opened the door, sat on his boot and wrapped herself around his leg.

"Good morning, little one." He tousled her hair and stepped carefully inside with her still attached to his leg.

"I puppy." Hannah crawled away on all fours.

He took one of Tess's hands and stroked her palm with his thumb. "How are you feeling about… everything?"

His touch broadened her smile, and if that wasn't enough to answer his question, she wrapped her arms around his waist and tipped her face up for a quick kiss. "I'm great."

His chest moved against hers with a breath he must have been holding. "Good."

"Now, will you tell me where we're going today?"

He held her tighter and kissed her again. "I told you it's a surprise. Patience, please."

"I'll try." With a pat on his firm backside, she spun away to gather her purse, the sparkly, pink backpack and her excited child. "If we're taking your truck we'll need to move her car seat."

After shifting her booster into the back seat of his double-cab truck, they headed out of town and farther into the Hill Country. Rolling pastures dotted the spaces between the hills and patches of trees. The sun shone clear and bright, lightening her heart and making anything seem possible. "Are there lots of wildflowers in the spring?"

"Tons." He briefly glanced her way before turning back to the winding road before them. "You'll love it."

A rush of disappointment slipped in to dampen her mood. They wouldn't be here when spring arrived. But that didn't mean they couldn't come for a visit.

Over a hill and around a sharp curve, Anson turned on his blinker and pulled slowly up to an ornate metal gate. It was flanked by a large limestone wall and stood open, hanging askew on its supports. Ironwork letters read Barton Estate, and beside that was a temporary sign on a wooden stake with metallic streamers.

Tess sucked in a breath. "Are you taking us to an estate sale?"

"I am. After seeing the way you like antiques and enjoyed the tour of Nan's house, I thought you might like this."

"You thought right."

He pulled through the gate and down an overgrown, tree-lined road. The asphalt was rutted with weed growth creeping into its crumbling surface. The mixture of oaks, crape myrtles and elms created a canopy over sections of the long, winding driveway.

He reached across the console and stroked her arm. "This is a place many have wanted to see and few have gotten into since the mid-1990s. Mrs. Barton became a bit of a recluse in her later years. She recently died with only two nephews as heirs."

"Are they selling the whole estate or just the contents of the house?"

"Everything."

"It's..." The enormous antebellum-style house came into view. "Wow. What a fabulous house."

He parked his big truck beside several others with attached trailers. "Looks like some people have come ready to buy a lot of big items."

"Probably antique dealers. I want to see everything." She unbuckled her seat belt and opened her door before he'd even turned off the truck.

He chuckled. "Somebody's excited."

"I really am."

Hannah woke when Anson unbuckled her seat. "Where we at?"

"A place your momma is very excited about." He turned around so she could climb on piggyback style. "Looks like the two of us will need to be very patient while she inspects the whole lot."

"Lot?" Hannah asked and clung to his neck.

Tess chuckled and walked beside them. "You know how I like to go in those stores with all of the old things? It's kind of like that. So, you'll need to be a big girl and use your eyes to look and not touch."

"I big girl." She giggled when Anson bounced her.

They stood at the end of a long brick pathway that arched gracefully around the curve of a hill and led to a grand front door. Six two-story columns stretched across the front, holding up the balcony over the large porch. Even with peeling white paint and overgrown landscaping, it took Tess's breath away.

"I see why people have been wanting to get a look around this estate."

"I came here a few times when I was a child. Nan brought me to the last few summer garden parties that were thrown here. She made me wear fancy, itchy clothes, but they had the best cookies I'd ever eaten."

"Better than the double chocolate chip cookies Nan makes?"

"That is them. I sweet-talked Mrs. Barton into giving Nan the recipe."

"Yep, I knew it. You've always been a charmer. I would've loved coming to parties here when I was a little girl."

Hannah wiggled on his back. "Go, Momma."

Tess realized she'd come to a complete stop, lost in admiring the house and grounds. "Okay. Let's go see it up close."

"What are you hoping to find?" Anson asked.

"I'd love to find a bedroom set. And a few end tables. Oh, and bookcases."

"I should've borrowed a trailer."

"We'll see." She smoothed her hand over the worn pedestal at the corner of the front steps. "I can control myself. Maybe." She shot him a sideways glance and grinned. "I'll make sure any purchases will fit in the bed of your truck."

"I'm sure we can handle whatever you buy." He knelt on the porch so Hannah could climb off his back.

"Hold, pease." She took each of them by a hand, and with her in the middle, they went in through the open door and moved to the center of a large front parlor.

Tess let the nostalgia of the surroundings wash over her senses and shared a smile with Anson. "I wouldn't have guessed you go to estate sales."

"I've never been to one, until now. I just thought it might be something you'd like."

Her chest squeezed as his sexy smile turned tender. Anson was the total opposite of Brent. She'd begged her ex to go to antique auctions in Boston, but he'd swiftly declined and took no interest in her passion for history, or anything she liked. She leaned across her daughter and kissed his cheek. "Thanks for thinking of me."

The fingers of his free hand slid up the back of

her scalp, and he pressed his lips to hers. "You're welcome, honey."

Someone sucked in a shocked breath and pulled Tess's attention to their left. A beautiful, dark-haired woman stared at them and whispered to the older lady beside her.

Anson brushed his hand down Tess's arm, and when she tried to step away, he clasped her fingers in his. "Morning, Mrs. Suarez. Nice to see you again, Shelby."

"You, too." Shelby nodded curtly, flicked a quick glance over Tess and pulled Mrs. Suarez along behind her.

"Old girlfriend?" Tess asked, once the other women had left the room.

"One date," he whispered out of the side of his mouth. "I kind of started making excuses about not having any free time after that."

"Look, Momma. Toys."

She followed the direction of her daughter's extended finger to the adjoining room. Several hobbyhorses, a wooden train set, china dolls, and all manner of blocks, books and other old toys filled one corner of a room.

"I remember that train set," Anson said. "Let's check out the toys and let your momma do some shopping."

"Play!" Hannah cheered and headed for the colorful spread of treasures.

He winked at Tess. "Go have fun. We'll entertain ourselves right here."

Her cheeks were beginning to ache from smiling, but she wouldn't trade the feeling for the world. "Keep a close eye on her, and please don't let her break anything."

"You got it."

Tess went to check out the kitchen and the dining room, but the furniture was not the style she was looking for. She always got a tingling sensation when a piece of furniture was right, but nothing gave her that burst of excitement she searched for.

Before going upstairs, she went back to check on Anson and Hannah. She ended up peeking around the corner and watching them for several minutes. They'd built block towers and a whole town around the old train set. No batteries or electricity was required, just imagination and willing hands to power the toys. She couldn't resist pulling out her phone and taking pictures of the two of them, lost in pretend with toys older than any of them.

Suddenly overcome with emotion, she ducked into an alcove and pressed her fingers against her eyes, willing the tears to stay away. Seeing Anson and Hannah together—like father and child—made her want to fall in love and run away all at the same time.

Anson and Hannah finished packing the train set in its wooden box. They put it and a china baby doll she'd picked out behind the cashier's table and set out to find Tess. The place had become crowded, so he picked her up and settled her on his hip.

"I'm getting hungry. What about you, little one?"

"I hungry. I see Momma." Hannah pointed.

The woman who occupied his thoughts stood in front of a table covered with boxes and trays of jewelry. One of his off-duty officers stood behind the table keeping an eye on the goods. Tess intently studied something in a purple velvet box. A smile spread across her face and brightened her eyes as she stroked its contents. Whatever it was, she appeared to love it.

"Hi, Momma," Hannah squealed.

"Hello, sweetie. Are you two finished playing?"

"Yes. Eat, pease."

"We're hungry," Anson added unnecessarily. "And we each picked out something to buy and put them up front." He nodded to the man behind the jewelry table. "How's it going, Jake?"

"Good, Chief. Just picking up a few extra bucks this weekend."

Anson made introductions, then turned his attention back to Tess. "Looks like you found something you like."

She looked at the box cradled in her hands and sighed. "Nothing that I need."

"Oooh, shiny," Hannah exclaimed and wiggled to get down.

"It's gorgeous," she agreed, and put it back on the table, then pulled several tags from her back pocket.

"I have a few items to pay for, then we can go eat. I need to get some moving blankets, then come back for everything. They said they'd hold it until tomorrow if needed."

"I'm pretty sure we have what you'll need for padding in the garage." When Tess and Hannah turned and walked hand in hand toward the front, he leaned across the table to whisper to Jake. "I want that necklace. Make sure it's set aside for me."

"You got it, Chief." Jake gave him a knowing grin, closed the velvet box and put it under the table.

Tess paid for a glass-front barrister bookcase, an Eastlake wall-mount shelf and a three-tiered side table. He insisted on paying for Hannah's doll. They made arrangements to come back the following day to pick up her new treasures.

Anson sat across from the girls at The Acorn Cafe. The Saturday lunch crowd was large today, and he'd requested a booth near the back and out of the heavy traffic areas. "What's everyone hungry for?"

"Ice cream." Hannah wiggled in her booster seat.

Tess moved the silverware from the reach of her daughter's dancing arms. "You have to eat something healthy for lunch, then we can order dessert."

"If you eat your lunch, maybe your momma will agree to going to The Sweet Cream Shop across the square."

"I've seen that place and thought about taking Hannah there for a treat."

"They have the best banana splits."

"Nana spit? What that?" Hannah scrunched up her nose, making both adults laugh.

He leaned forward like he had a very important secret. "A banana split is an ice cream dessert with three scoops of vanilla ice cream topped with strawberry, chocolate and pineapple with whipped cream, pecans and a cherry on top."

Her little eyes had grown wide as she listened. "Yummy."

"Tess Harper, you haven't introduced her to banana splits?"

"Guilty. They're so big. It's always seemed like too much for only the two of us."

Something he couldn't name flashed in her expression before she quickly masked her pain with a smile. He reached across the table and took her hand, wishing for a way to soothe her wounds and show her the kind of love she and her daughter deserved. "If we share one today, we'll each get our own scoop. And Hannah can have the cherry."

She squeezed his fingers. "That sounds nice."

Throughout the meal, several people stopped to say hello and meet Oak Hollow's newest residents. Other folks stared at the three of them with varying degrees of speculation in their gazes. He was thankful their waiter was a high school boy and not the waitress that always flirted and unbuttoned the top of her uniform.

When they'd finished, he went up to the counter to pay. "Hey, Dawn. Business is booming today."

"It is. And it looks like you're having a good day as well. Any chance of wedding bells in your future?"

A rush of heat warmed his skin, and he suddenly liked the idea of the girls being thought of as his. "That's Tess and Hannah Harper. They're new in town, and they rent my house."

"You look at her the way Sam looks at me." She smiled at her husband through the opening to the kitchen.

Anson took a deep breath and wondered if everyone could read him like this observant woman. "Unfortunately, they're only staying in town for a few months." His good mood suddenly dipped. He didn't like thinking about the fact that they were leaving.

Unless...I can change her mind.

Chapter Eleven

Morning came too soon, as most Mondays do. Tess slapped at her alarm and pulled the pillow over her head, blocking out the watery sunlight filtering through the blinds. Even though she loved her work, forcing herself out of a warm bed was a chore. If Anson was still in her bed, it would be much easier—and way more fun—to wake up. Which one of them would wake first? And what wonderfully creative methods could she use to bring a smile to his expressive mouth?

The night before, Anson had dressed and slipped from her bed in the late hours. She understood his fear of leaving his grandmother alone overnight, and she knew keeping some level of distance between them would be better in the long run. His staying all night would only make their relationship feel more serious, but she couldn't help wishing things were different. Wishing she was different and her heart was whole and capable of fully opening to loving another man. She was treading in dangerous territory, but even with continued warnings to herself, she had no desire to pull back from what they had going on.

Her alarm clock blared again, and she stopped daydreaming and flung back the covers. After the coffee was brewing, she crawled into bed beside Hannah and rubbed her back.

"Time to get up, sweetie pie." Her little one stretched and sighed but didn't open her eyes. "Hannah Lynn, you have a playdate with Jenny's cousin today."

Hannah popped up onto her knees, rubbed her eyes and then scrambled from the bed. "I play."

Tess's heart squeezed as she held her breath and sent up a silent prayer the playdate would be a success. She loved seeing her baby girl excited, but there was always the fear of another child's rejection. Tess knew all too well how much rejection could hurt. But she didn't think Jenny would have suggested getting the little girls together if she didn't think Katie would be receptive to playing with Hannah. And she supposed every parent, no matter if their child was special needs or not, had to deal with such fears.

Hannah climbed back onto the bed, jumped a few times and bounced onto her bottom. "Up, Momma."

"Okay. Let's have cereal and toast for breakfast. That's quick." She swung her legs off the bed and let her daughter pretend to pull her to her feet. "You're so strong."

They stepped out of their front door into the cool November breeze. The morning sun peeked through a thick layer of clouds, and the day was cold enough for jackets.

"My kitty cat." Hannah tiptoed farther into Nan's yard, sensing the skittish tomcat might bolt if she moved too fast.

She gave her daughter a moment to coax Tom-Tom over for one brief scratch on the head before he ran behind a bush. Hannah ran ahead as usual, but this time she rang the bell and waited for the door to open.

Tess stood back and watched Anson greeting Hannah. He clasped her under the arms and gave her one of those gentle tosses into the air that made her squeal with delight. The second she was back on her feet, she darted past him and into the house.

He adjusted the holster on his belt and gave Tess a pantie-melting smile. "Good morning, beautiful."

"'Morning." She stepped into the foyer and couldn't resist looking him over from head to toe. The man definitely knew how to wear a uniform and make it look hot, but the sight of his armed utility belt prodded her phobia that she'd lose the people she loved. That tucked-away place inside her that remembered seeing her father leave for work in a similar uniform and never come home again.

He closed the distance between them and took her hands in a way that had so quickly become natural between them. "I'm glad I got to see you before work. You okay this morning? You have that little crease between your brows."

In an attempt to hide her worry, she looked at their joined hands. "Just tired, and I missed you when I woke up." *Crap. Why did I say that? He's going to think I'm pushing for something more.*

He tugged her closer until she wrapped her arms around his neck. "One morning very soon, I'd like to wake up beside you like I did when we were sick."

"Guess you need to get sick again."

His features twisted comically, and he groaned. "Can't I just fake it?"

"Sure. I'll never tell. We can play doctor." She rested her head on his chest, enjoying the vibration of his laugh against her cheek.

The old wooden floor creaked under someone's weight, and they both turned to see Nan grinning at them.

"Good morning," Tess said, cheeks warming under the observation.

"'Morning, dear. Anson, you do not need to be here every night. I am perfectly capable of sleeping in my own house without a babysitter."

"Guess you heard our conversation?" he asked unnecessarily.

"Some of it."

"Oh God," Tess grumbled, and rubbed her face.

Nan chuckled. "There's no need for embarrassment. I'm the one who's been encouraging the two of you. It makes me happy to see young people enjoying life. Have a good day at work," she said to her grandson, then turned and headed back toward the kitchen.

Tess punched his arm when he laughed. "I'm so mortified," she whispered. "I can't believe she heard me making sexual innuendos."

"She's fairly modern-minded for her age."

"We're not going to get a lecture about premarital sex, or sleeping with someone you've known such a short time?"

"No. Since she approves of you, we're all good."

Her brows winged up. "Have there been others she's tried to run off?"

"Yeah, my ex-wife, but as it turns out, she had good reasons. Nan saw things right away that I didn't." The radio on his belt beeped, and voices talked about a fender bender on Main Street. "I better go. I'll see you this evening?"

"You know where to find me." She smoothed the front of his shirt. "Be safe."

"Always." He kissed her once more, then went out the door.

Tess rubbed her lips, still tingling from his kiss. She made her way to the kitchen and found her daughter and Nan sitting at the table talking about puppies.

"Jenny and Katie should be here any minute," Nan said.

As if on cue, they heard the front door open and little feet running across the wooden floor.

She held her breath while Jenny introduced the girls. There was always that moment of waiting to see how another child would react to her daughter.

Katie's big smile never wavered, and she held out a bag stuffed with toys. "Want to see my dolls?"

Hannah nodded, and the two of them left the kitchen.

Tess blew out a breath and smiled at their retreating backs.

"Don't worry," Jenny said. "They'll be fine, and I'll keep a close eye on them."

"Thank you. Don't hesitate to call me for any reason."

"I won't." Jenny began unloading a bag of groceries and putting items into the refrigerator. "I'll have lunch ready when you and Nan get back from the quilt shop."

Tess drove one street over from the town square to a blue-and-white Craftsman house with a big sign that read Queen's Sew N Sew. Today's agenda was picking out quilts for display at the museum and gathering stories to go along with them.

"I've never seen a fabric store in such a wonderful location."

"It's very unique," Nan said. "You'll really like the Queen Mothers. We've been sewing together for almost thirty years. This will be the first time I've met with them since my stroke."

"I'm glad I could bring you today. Wait there and I'll come around to your side and help you out."

Nan put a hand on her arm before she could open the door. "Anson was right. I let myself get the blues and wasn't trying very hard to get better. Without my Isaac…" She shook her head. "What I'm really trying to say is that having you and Hannah around has reminded me there's still a lot left for me to live for."

Tess could see the longing for lost love in every line and wrinkle of her face. "I'm so glad we could be a positive influence. You seem to be recovering quickly."

"It wasn't that I physically couldn't get up and do things. I just didn't have the motivation. Dr. Clark told me I was depressed, and I refused to believe him, but maybe he was right."

Tess patted her hand. "It can be a hard thing to admit. I've been through it myself."

"I know you have, my dear. Let's you and I keep reminding each other about all the happiness yet to come in our lives."

"That's a deal I'll gladly accept."

Once they returned to the house with six quilts, they found Hannah and Katie having a tea party.

Their precious giggles made Tess smile and lightened some of the worry weighing on her heart.

Nan invited Tess to look through her cedar-lined storage closet for items to use for the "display through time" exhibit. More like a small room than a closet, it smelled of cedar and lavender sachets. It was well organized with a section of hanging garments, trunks and various storage boxes covering a wall of shelves.

"Could you get that long pink-and-white box?" Nan asked.

Tess lifted down the dress box from a top shelf, carried it into Nan's bedroom and placed it on her bed. Under layers of acid-free tissue paper rested a beautiful ivory satin wedding gown. A uniquely angled neckline and simple adornment created an elegant design, that resulted in the most exquisite dress she'd ever seen.

"Oh, it's lovely. I knew I liked it from your black-and-white wedding photos, but in person it's so much better."

Nan sat on the bed and lightly stroked a line of tiny satin buttons on one sleeve of the gown. "I wish you could've seen the rest of my wedding in color. The reception was in this backyard. It was his parents' house at the time. There were oodles of early spring flowers and my bouquet was pale pink rosebuds. Isaac wore a gray suit and was the most handsome man I'd ever seen. Anson looks a lot like him."

Tess lay back on the bed and closed her eyes. She

could almost smell the flowers and hear the happy chatter as she lost herself in Nan's vivid retelling of one of the happiest days of her life.

"There was even a quartet playing music throughout the evening. Our first dance was on the grass, but that didn't stop Isaac from twirling me around and making me feel like a princess."

"That sounds amazing."

"Try it on, dear."

Tess propped up on her elbow. "Oh, I couldn't." *But I really want to.*

"Of course you can. You're taller than me, but I think it will fit."

"Okay, let's give it a try."

She undressed down to her bra and panties, and Nan helped her slip the sleek, satin gown over her head. The soft fabric slid over her skin like the touch of a lover. She and Nan glanced up into the full-length mirror and both sucked in a breath.

"Oh, my dear. You are so striking." The older woman clasped her hands against her chest and smiled.

A knot formed in Tess's throat and tears pricked the backs of her eyes. She'd never thought to see herself in a wedding dress again. Especially one that made her feel so beautiful. Panic rose in her chest, challenging her decision never to consider marriage again.

"Thank you for letting me try it on. I should take it off before I get it dirty."

Before I get any ideas about wearing it for real.

* * *

Tess sat on the back porch with Nan, while Anson and Hannah played under the magnolia tree. He hadn't even had a chance to take off his uniform before her daughter took him by the hand and insisted on showing him something.

A brisk breeze gusted across the porch and Tess wrapped her sweater a little tighter around herself. "Tomorrow I'll go through my notes and write up all the stories you and the ladies told me today. Will you read over them once I'm done and make sure I didn't miss anything?"

"I'd love to." The older woman shifted to face Tess. "Thank you for coming to Oak Hollow."

"Of course. I'm enjoying the work. Having you and a hardworking group of people in the historical society has been a big help."

"Not just for taking this job. I want to thank you for coming into all of our lives. As I said earlier, you and Hannah have gotten me off my tired old bum and back to the business of living. And you've made Anson smile again. His real smile."

Tess cleared the emotion from her throat. "You've both made a difference in our lives as well."

Nan waved a hand at her grandson and Hannah both crouched down under the tree. "Look at the two of them. So sweet. Did you tell him about Hannah's surgery yet?"

"No. I'll tell him tonight after she goes to sleep."

"That's good. And you two have got to stop worrying about someone always being with me. I'm more than capable of being home alone overnight," she said with extra emphasis.

Tess was growing used to her saying things like this, and it no longer totally shocked her.

"I always keep this alert thing around my neck," Nan continued. "I'll push the button if I need anything and help will come running. You young folks need to enjoy and live your life without worrying about me all the time. I should lock Anson out of the house tonight."

Tess chuckled. "I doubt a lock would keep him from coming in to check on you."

"Well, you know what I'm getting at."

"Yes, I think I do."

Hannah ran up onto the porch and stopped in front of Nan. "We make flowers?"

"If we send Anson and your momma to the garden center to pick up some pansies, we can plant a few in some pots." She looked at her watch. "They're open for another hour."

Hannah bounced up and down on her toes. "Go, Momma. Flowers."

"Are we going somewhere?" Anson asked as he joined them on the porch and took a seat on the swing beside Tess.

"Yes," Nan said. "I need you and Tess to go to the garden center. Hannah and I want to plant pansies."

He returned his grandmother's smile. "I'm happy to hear you feel like working in your garden again."

"I've been doing all those exercises they told me to do, and I'm getting around just fine without my walker. You have got to stop hovering over me all the time. Dr. Clark said my blood work looks good. I'm all better now."

Anson shared a smile with Tess and put his arm around her shoulders. "Message received, but I'm not going to stop worrying about you until you stop worrying about me."

"Anson Curry. I'm your grandmother, and I will never stop worrying about you. It's my job. You, however, need to worry about your own future."

As Anson drove them to Green Forest Nursery, she stared out the window at the passing houses, businesses and stretches of nature dotted with drifting leaves and swaying trees. Falling for a man was something that had definitely not been in her plans. Neither had falling for this whimsical, small Texas town that pulled her in deeper with its charms every day. Leaving after Christmas wasn't going to be as easy as she'd thought. She sighed and pressed her forehead against the cold window.

"What's wrong, honey?"

She flashed a quick smile, attempting to guard her worrisome thoughts. "Nothing."

"Not buying it."

"Just thinking about a few things Nan and I were talking about."

"She tends to be full of advice, whether the listener wants to hear it or not. I'm sorry if she upset you."

"No, no. She didn't." *Just made me think about things I shouldn't.*

He stopped at a red light and looked at her. "Care to elaborate?"

"We talked about moving to Houston."

A swallow ran visibly down his throat, and he shifted his gaze back on the road. "Is your next job a big one?"

"Well… I haven't actually accepted one, yet. But I've heard back from two places and they're both terrific opportunities."

"I see. I guess money can be tight when you're a single mom."

She tucked one foot under her leg and studied his clenched jaw and the crease that appeared between his brows. He deserved her honesty. "I suppose most do, but I don't actually have to work. I just really like what I do. I got a large settlement in the divorce."

Anson winced at the stab of pain her confession caused. *Guess she just doesn't want to stay here.* "I see."

"We have to go to Houston because Hannah is having open heart surgery in early January."

His muscles tensed and his own heart jerked in his chest, and he was glad he'd already pulled into a parking spot. Tess jumped out of his truck before he could form words into an appropriate response. He climbed out and quickly caught up to her. "Honey, wait."

"Let's just get these flowers and get back before Jenny has to leave."

He stepped in front of her and gently caught her shoulders before she ran into him. "Talk to me. Please."

"It's…" She cleared her throat, swallowed hard and shook her head. "Talking about it makes it so real."

He pulled her into a hug, and it only took a few seconds for her to relax against him. If they weren't in public, he'd tumble her into bed and make her forget her worries, but that would have to wait until they were alone. And until he found out more about what was going on with Hannah needing surgery. The least he could do was to give her a minute to compose her thoughts. They stood in the gravel parking lot, locked in a tight embrace, not saying a word.

A group of three women walked past, staring and whispering behind their hands. All of them were persistent members of the "Pantie Posse," and he knew the rumor mill would pick up speed. He'd be the talk of the town in a matter of minutes. Possibly seconds. And he hoped Tess wouldn't be upset if she heard any of it. She was a private person and breaking through her tough barriers was challenge enough. But a challenge he'd decided he was prepared to meet. At least he thought so.

The other ladies' intense observations did not

make him release his hold on Tess. Instead, he held her tighter and kissed the top of her head. Maybe this would make them back off from their relentless pursuits.

Take the hint, ladies.

"Tess, honey, you don't have to say anything right now. You can tell me all about it when we're alone. When you're ready." He reluctantly released her and, with a hand on the small of her back, he guided her inside the garden center. "Let's get those petunias."

"Pansies. Petunias don't do as well in the winter." She slid her hand along his forearm and laced her fingers with his. "And the cold snap that blew in this afternoon is a strong one."

The warmth and tenderness of her touch soothed some of the disquiet that always lay waiting inside him, and the rapid pulse in her wrist fluttered against his own. "You know about gardening, too?"

"Only a bit."

"I think you know quite a bit about a lot of things. You're one smart lady." He liked the way that got a smile to return to her plump mouth.

"And you are a smart man for recognizing it. I like smart men."

"Lucky me." He raised their joined hands and kissed the back of her knuckles.

They filled a rolling cart with purple and yellow flowers, paid and then loaded them into the bed of his truck. The cold in the air chilled their skin and it felt good to climb back into the cab.

"You know we're going to end up helping Hannah and Nan plant these," she said, and rubbed her hands together.

He grinned and turned on the heated seats. "I figured as much. I'm just glad Nan is even considering working in the greenhouse again. You and Little One have been exactly what she needed." He leaned across the console and crooked a finger until she came close enough to press his lips to hers. "And what I needed."

"You scare me, Chief Anson Curry. Be gentle with me. Please." She twined her fingers into his hair, and in a not so gentle tug, she pulled him closer and deepened the kiss.

Anson's head swam with her taste. Her warmth. The confession of her fears. It meant she was opening up and letting him in, at least a little bit. But a little bit at a time could lead to something beautiful between them.

Don't break my heart, sweet Tess.

Chapter Twelve

Hannah was so excited when they returned that they planted one tray of flowers into pots before cold and darkness sent them indoors for Nan's homemade hot chocolate. Tess sat with Nan at the breakfast table while Anson and Hannah looked for marshmallows in the butler's pantry.

"This is the most delicious hot chocolate I've ever had." Tess inhaled the fragrant steam and took another sip of the sweet yet subtly spicy drink. "There's a flavor to it that I can't put my finger on."

"The recipe was passed down to me from my own grandmother, Beatrice," Nan said.

"Is it a secret family recipe?"

"It is at that." Nan's smile held a playful note and

there was a hopeful gleam in her pale blue eyes. "Maybe I can share it with you one day soon."

Is she hinting that she wants me to be part of her family?

Anson came out of the pantry with Hannah bouncing on his hip. "We found the marshmallows."

"I find." Hannah pointed to her chest.

"She's right," he said. "They were way down on a low shelf, just at this little one's eye level."

She giggled when he tickled her tummy, then flung her arms around his neck, squashing the bag of marshmallows between them. "I wuv you."

"Love you, too."

Tess jerked and sloshed hot chocolate on the table. Nan was right—Hannah had already bonded with Anson. And so had she. Leaving Oak Hollow would not be a casual so long and goodbye like the other places they'd been. Leaving Anson and Nan and this town was guaranteed to be difficult. She met his eyes, emotion clear on his face, but she couldn't pinpoint what he was feeling about her daughter's declaration of love.

He patted Hannah on the back once more, then put her on her feet, opened the bag of mini marshmallows. "How many in your cup, little one?"

"Five, free, one, two," she said and held up four fingers.

He counted aloud as he dropped one at a time into her mug, then sat beside Tess and kissed her cheek. "Some sugar for her momma, too."

Tess leaned against his shoulder and lifted her lips to his cheek. She suddenly had a mighty sweet tooth.

Anson received a phone call from the police station, and while he solved whatever problem needed his attention, she took Hannah home for a bath and took a quick shower herself. He arrived at their house with wet hair, dressed in faded jeans and a T-shirt just as they finished their first bedtime story.

"You late," Hannah scolded, and yawned.

"Sorry, little one. Are you too tired for one more story?"

With one more jaw-cracking yawn, she handed him a book. Three pages into the story she was softly snoring.

"Sweet dreams, baby girl," Tess whispered and tucked the blanket around her daughter's shoulders. She caught Anson staring at her butt as they slipped from the bedroom. "See something interesting?"

"What can I say?" His mischievous grin appeared. "You look really good in yoga pants."

The compliment brought a flutter to her stomach. "I brought in wood for a fire. How are you at building one?"

"I got this." He headed straight for the fireplace. "I was an Eagle Scout."

"Of course you were." Tess grinned and grabbed a chocolate cupcake, opened a beer for Anson and poured herself a glass of red wine. With her feet propped on the coffee table, she marveled at Anson's proficiency with wood and matches. In no time, red-orange flames cast his large frame in silhouette, and his blond hair glowed like it was lit from within. He reminded her of an ancient warrior kneeling before a campfire. Her mouth went dry and she stood, drawn closer to the vision before her.

I'm going to remember this moment forever. "I love staring into the flames when the logs have turned to glowing embers. It's kind of like watching the clouds to see what shapes form and morph into new ones."

"I do the same thing." The metal poker clanged against its stand as he set it back in place, then rose to his feet. "Let's move the couch closer so we can get a better view."

Body temperature rising, she wrapped her arms around his waist. "You continue to surprise me with your thoughtfulness." The soft tickle of his breath on her neck sent a wave of sensation across her skin.

"It's easy when we enjoy a lot of the same things." He rubbed a hand along her spine and swayed to the slow beat of the song playing on the stereo.

"You didn't take me to an estate sale because it was something *you* wanted to do."

"True. But once we got there, I had a lot of fun. I even got a new toy."

She chuckled. "You can try to deny it all you want, but I know the truth, Chief Curry. You are thoughtful and protective and sweet." She slid her hands under the front of his T-shirt, teasing her fingers over taut skin and hard muscles, and wished it was her lips on his skin. "And sexy."

A deep moan rumbled in his chest. "You're about to start another kind of fire."

"A little anticipation can be a good thing." She kissed his neck to prove her point. "Let's put that plan of yours into action and move the couch closer to the fireplace."

"Yes, ma'am."

They shifted the furniture, shared the cupcake and settled in to fire-gaze with his head on her lap.

The spicy wine tingled on her tongue, and his short hair tickled her fingertips as she massaged his scalp. Contentment was a breath of fresh air in the stifling box she'd kept herself tucked safely inside of for too many years.

He turned his head and kissed her stomach. "Will you tell me about the day Hannah was born?"

A rush of tightly held memories slipped out of hiding. These were normally things she didn't let herself think about in the presence of others, but Tess suddenly had the urge to share more about her and Hannah's life. She closed her eyes and allowed the stream of emotions to wash over her. Great joy at the birth of her precious girl mingled with a touch of sorrow for the loss of the baby that every parent expects. The one with ten fingers and toes, and the correct number of chromosomes.

"I've never told the whole story to anyone. Bits and pieces of it here and there, but never all of the details. I guess when you have family, you probably tell the story over and over. Whether it's your forty-eight-hour labor or emergency C-section. But I didn't have any family waiting to hear my story. I just sort of sealed it away inside like a secret that was only mine and Hannah's."

"Tess, honey, I'm sorry. I don't mean to—"

"No." She stopped him from saying more with a hand on his cheek. "If you'll listen, I think I'd like to tell it."

He cradled his much larger hand over hers and turned his head to kiss the well of her palm. "I'll listen. Happily."

She took one more fortifying gulp of wine and set her glass back onto the table beside his beer. "I had rented a small studio apartment near the hospital in Worcester. Lots of the medical residents and staff lived there, and I'd made casual friends with a few of them. The afternoon I went into labor, I grabbed my packed bag and started walking to the hospital."

He sat up and his expression went almost comical. "You walked while you were in labor?"

"Yep. Not my best idea."

"You didn't have…" He hesitated before continuing. "No one went with you?"

"A friend from grad school had planned to be with me, but her father died and she'd flown to Washington for his funeral. The hospital wasn't far from my apartment, but I only got part of the way. The pains started coming much faster and harder than I had expected." When he unfolded the fingers of her clenched fist, she realized she'd tensed at the memory of pains.

"What did you do?"

"Luckily there was no shortage of medical professionals walking along. One of them flagged down a taxi. The driver was worried my water would break in his car, but the nurse with me assured him that rarely happened. Just as I was getting out of the car at the hospital entrance, it happened. I leaned forward and a rush of fluid appeared along with a killer contraction. The driver shook his hands toward heaven and said something in a Russian accent."

Anson chuckled, then caught himself and grimaced. "Sorry. I'm sure it wasn't funny at the time."

"It kind of was. I even laughed in between gasping and being totally mortified. I handed the driver extra cash and got into the wheelchair they'd rushed out to the car." Tess shivered as his hand moved along her thigh. She placed her palm across his knuckles and laced their fingers, grateful for the comfort. "I bet he still tells that story about me defiling his taxicab."

"It's probably developed into you actually giving birth in the back seat."

"No doubt. By the time I was admitted, I felt a new pressure and fullness way down low. An overwhelming urge to push. I was holding myself above the seat of the wheelchair for fear her head would come out and I'd sit on her. As I was shifting onto the bed, I told a nurse to check me because I had the urge to push." Tess reached for her wine and swirled it before taking a sip. "The nurse continued to write in my chart and didn't believe me. I wanted to fly across the room banshee-style when she told me it would be many hours before I was ready to push."

He took the glass from her and drank the last sip. "I'm guessing it didn't take hours?"

"Definitely not. I had a sixth sense I should *not* allow myself to push. I panted instead, and braced myself on the bed rails in agony. Another nurse came in, and I yelled something about no one listening and checking to see if the head was coming out. When she finally pulled back the sheet, her eyes got huge and panic was clear on her face. She started barking orders and a doctor rushed in." Tess shivered and tucked her hands under her arms. Her delivery room had then become chaotic and loud. And terrifying.

Anson tugged her onto his lap and pressed his forehead to hers. "Take your time, honey."

His breath was warm against her lips, and she couldn't resist closing the distance for a kiss. He tasted of spicy red wine, tinged with chocolate from the cupcake they'd shared. When she pulled back, the fire in his expression gave her the strength to finish. "I want to tell you the rest. I need to say it aloud."

"And I'd like to hear it." They settled into a comfortable position with her head tucked under his chin.

"The doctor told me to push, and I did, but it was such an odd feeling that I gasped and let up. Someone yelled that I had to do better, and I immediately pushed again, much harder. Hannah's heart was showing signs of distress. He held up forceps and told me I got one more chance before he used them." She couldn't control the tremble that coursed through her body.

Anson held her a little tighter and pressed his lips against her forehead.

Telling her story was turning out to be very therapeutic. He had a way of showing her he was truly listening and cared about what she was saying. She took a moment to inhale his woodsy musk, then continued. "Some protective instinct hit me, and I decided in a millisecond that I would rip myself into pieces before I'd let him wrap those giant metal spoons around my baby's head. I bore down with all my strength. Thankfully, she came out seconds later."

"Did she cry right away?"

The memory evoked a sharp ache in her throat and tension in her chest. "No. She didn't make a sound, and it was terrifying. Instead of having that magical moment where they place your newborn on your chest, they whisked her away to the other side of the room and started working on her. Her skin had a bluish tinge, and she wasn't moving or crying. I thought I'd die right then and there with her. It was probably only a few seconds, but it felt like a lifetime before I heard her first cry."

Anson let out a shuddering breath. "I bet that was a huge relief."

"More than I can even begin to express. I asked to

see her, and the same bitchy nurse that had already gotten on my bad side came over and said the doctor should talk to me before I saw my baby. I told her I needed to see and hold my daughter. She argued, saying a doctor needed to prepare me."

Anson raised a brow and pried her fingernails from his wrist.

"Oh crap. I'm sorry I hurt you." She rubbed the grooves her nails had made in his flesh.

"It's fine. Why was she keeping Hannah from you?"

"She didn't realize I already knew about the Down syndrome. Even with someone still working between my legs I tried to get up. I don't think I had even finished delivering the afterbirth yet. When Nurse Ratched argued with me, I told the room at large to get her out before I called my lawyer."

"You have a lawyer?"

"No." She grinned up at him. "It was an empty threat, but it worked."

Anson nipped her chin with his teeth. "You are a mighty momma bear. I wish I had been there to see that."

I wish you were Hannah's father.

The thought came unbidden and startled her with a rush of longing, but she continued her retelling. "The nurse stormed from the room and moments later someone placed Hannah in my arms." Tears began to roll freely from Tess's eyes. "She was so tiny. Five pounds and twelve ounces. She blinked those big eyes at me, and her little rosebud mouth worked like she was ready to eat. A different nurse, a sweet one, helped me untie my gown and settle her against my breast. I only got a few minutes with her before they took her to the NICU. They did an echocardiogram and several other tests."

"So they knew from the beginning that she had a heart condition?"

"Yes. She was born with a congenital heart defect. I've always known she'd have open heart surgery at some point. They thought she'd need surgery before her first birthday, but we've been able to hold it off longer than they first predicted. She's done really well for the most part."

"I'm sure it has something to do with the wonderful care you give her."

"It hasn't been me alone. She's had lots of great therapists for speech, physical therapy, feeding therapy and several others. I need to find new therapists, and I've already been looking into schools."

"In Houston?"

"Yes."

"When is her surgery?"

"January. I'll find out the exact date when I take her for an appointment in Houston a few days after Thanksgiving. I know the surgery is necessary, and I've had her whole life to prepare myself for it, but it scares the hell out of me. I dread the day they have to…cut open her chest. They'll have to stop my baby's heart in order to fix it."

Anson cupped her cheek and kissed her briefly. "You won't be alone this time. I'll be there for you and for Hannah at the hospital. I'll hold your hand through the whole thing. Or, if it suits you better, I'll be your punching bag."

"Punching bag?"

He shrugged and rubbed his thumb along her lower lip. "You know how sometimes when things get tough and all you want to do is hit something? If need be, I'll stand there and let you give me your best shot. Open my arms and let you fire away your fears and frustrations."

"That's quite an offer." She swung her feet to the floor and stood in front of him. "What if I want you to open your arms to me right now?"

Anson rose to his feet, long arms swept wide. An equally broad and very sexy smile spread across his chiseled face. "Fire away, honey."

They stood a breath apart. She took a second to admire him, then closed the distance and splayed both hands on his chest, recognizing the passion and tenderness that made this man unique. For the first time in her life, a man looked at her as if she'd hung the moon.

Locked in his embrace, their lips met in a fast hard kiss, screaming with the attraction they'd both been feeling since the day they'd met. His hands slid down to cup her hips then farther still to lift her up until she wrapped her legs around his waist.

With trembling hands, she wrestled off his T-shirt, anxious to touch his skin and feel him with nothing between them. "I'm in your custody. Take me to bed, Chief," she whispered against his ear, then nibbled his earlobe.

He shivered and moaned as he turned and headed down the short hallway. "You've got me under your spell, fairy princess." He paused at Hannah's door, peeked in, and a tender smile curved one corner of his lips before he continued down the hall.

Tess's heart opened to him even further. It might have been that he only wanted to make sure she was asleep and wouldn't interrupt them, but she thought it was more than that. More like he needed to make sure Hannah was safe before he could relax. Like he thought of her first, as a real father should do. She nuzzled her face against the warm column of his neck, inhaling his spicy scent.

He used his foot to close her bedroom door behind them.

Their desire shifted to a tender but still-urgent tension. His lust-filled blue eyes stared down at her, and she pushed his shirt from his broad shoulders, then kissed the pounding pulse point on his neck.

They were naked in seconds, but made love slowly, taking the time to appreciate every kiss. Every touch.

An hour later, they lay tangled together in happy contentment.

* * *

"Can I stay and hold you all night?" he whispered.

"I'd like that." *I'll need this memory to take with me when...*

Suddenly, she wanted to find a way to stay in Oak Hollow.

Chapter Thirteen

The town square bustled with lunchtime activity and early holiday shoppers. Pumpkins and fall leaf garlands remained, but the rest of the Halloween decorations had disappeared with the goblins and ghosts. Tess tilted her face to the sun as she walked back to the museum after inquiring about special needs programs at the elementary school. She'd instantly liked the early childhood teacher, Ms. Blake, but she'd keep that to herself for now. At least she knew the available options.

Just in case.

The savory aroma of food overlaid the earthy musk of fallen leaves blowing on the cool breeze.

Her stomach grumbled, but she didn't stop to eat. She picked up her pace instead, wanting to get back to the museum before Anson got there with the lunch he'd promised.

An older gentleman walked past and tipped his cowboy hat. "Afternoon, ma'am."

"Good afternoon." She kept walking, then caught the reflection of her smiling face in a store window. It was an odd feeling to be away from Hannah and calm at the same time. Built-in childcare was a benefit Tess hadn't expected when accepting the job in Oak Hollow. Not just because it gave her uninterrupted hours to work, but because it gave Hannah time with new people who cared about her. Having her child with people she trusted was a rare comfort.

She continued her short walk and hummed the song, "Keeper of the Stars."

Tess entered the museum, waved at the electrician and headed for the back room. There was a display case that needed to be prepped before it could be restained. It wasn't exactly part of her job description, but it was something she enjoyed doing. She turned on the radio, found a piece of sandpaper and worked while she waited for Anson.

A smile lifted the corners of her mouth, and for once, she didn't allow herself to worry about what-ifs or start envisioning the worst. She'd made the decision to allow herself some long-overdue, guilt-free fun. A bit of time to be a woman as well as a mother.

* * *

Anson shifted the bag of food and tray of drinks to open the museum door. Tess wasn't in sight, but he saw one of the local electricians. "Afternoon, Jim."

"Hey, Anson. What are you up to?"

"I brought lunch for Tess. Is she here?"

"Back room." Jim glanced at his watch. "Glad you came in. I'm supposed to meet my wife at the Acorn in fifteen minutes."

Anson followed the sound of country music coming from one of the back rooms and located the woman from his fantasies. The temptress was on her knees with a sanding block in one hand. He leaned against the doorframe and watched as she shifted, braced herself on her free hand, and sanded the old wood with steady strokes. Her tongue was caught between her teeth in concentration, and her butt swayed enticingly to the beat of the song.

He was going to need to adjust the fit of his pants at any moment. "I hope you're hungry." *Because I'm ravenous.*

She remained on her knees but glanced over her shoulder and shot him a sexy smile. "I'm starving."

He put the food and drinks on top of a desk, then pulled her to her feet and kissed her but kept it light and playful. Unfortunately, there was no door on the room, so sneaking in an afternoon quickie wasn't an option. He stepped away and pulled out two burgers and fries. "I have to work late tonight. I'm covering the end of a shift for another officer. It's his first anniversary and I told him he should take his wife out and not put it off till the weekend."

"That was nice, and rather romantic of you. How late is your shift?"

"Eleven."

"Need me to return the favor and bring supper to you later?"

"As much as I'd love the company, there's a big thunderstorm coming in this evening, and I don't want you and the little one out in the weather."

"Guess we'll just have to settle for a little stolen time right now." She hooked a finger in between the buttons of his uniform shirt and pulled him closer. "Kiss me again. Kiss me like you mean it."

He obligingly cupped the back of her head for a longer, deeper exploration than their hello kiss. Someone cleared their throat and they pulled apart.

One of the carpenters shifted from foot to foot and tried to keep the smile off his face. "Sorry to interrupt, but my boss is on the phone and needs to know what kind of wood you want ordered for that case we're building along the back wall." He held out his cell phone to Tess.

It took her a moment longer to shake off her embarrassment, find her voice and take the phone. "Thanks."

Soft spatters of rain tapped against the bedroom window as she read Hannah a bedtime story. By the time they'd finished two books and her daughter's eyes fluttered closed, lightning brightened the night sky, quickly followed by deep rumbles of thunder you could feel in your bones. Tess had always loved thunderstorms, especially falling asleep to the sound of rain rapping softly on the roof, but she couldn't sleep yet.

Her thoughts kept drifting back to the stories Nan shared when they'd pulled out her wedding dress. She wanted to hear more about Nan's life, especially her love story with Anson's grandfather. Writing a novel was Tess's secret dream, and her fingers itched to get on the keyboard and turn Nan's words into scenes that stirred emotions and came to life. It would make a wonderful book, but it wasn't her story to tell.

With a glass of wine, she settled on the couch with her laptop. If nothing else, she could write about his grandparents' wedding and display it in the museum beside her dress. It would be fun to write the happy parts, but sadness kept tugging on Tess's heart. Her glimpses into Nan's love story gave her an idea of why she'd struggled to recover after her stroke. Losing the love of her life had left a strong woman heartbroken and lonely. The pain she must have suffered after his death, no doubt still suffered, gave Tess pause about moving forward in her own romance. The friends with benefits arrangement she'd envisioned with Anson was evolving into more, and no matter how much she resisted...

I'm falling in love.

She set aside her laptop and paced the room, her pulse keeping tempo with the rapidly falling rain. He was definitely attracted to her, but he hadn't expressed long-term thoughts or feelings. Nan believed she and Hannah were what Anson needed. Was there a chance they could build a life in this town? Together?

Could he ever love me? Truly love me and Hannah and not want to leave us?

A sharp pain in her palm made her realize she clutched Hannah's new metal star badge as if it held the answers. She lifted it to stare at the shiny surface.

"Should I wish upon a star?"

Lightning flashed and thunder boomed so close that the windows rattled, and the electricity blinked out. Tess froze in place and clutched both hands and the badge against her leaping heart. "That must be a sign, but I don't know what it means."

She made her way down the hallway to Hannah's room, but her daughter still slept soundly. Light shone in the windows and she walked closer to peer into the night. Only her house had gone dark.

Tess rummaged in what she'd labeled the kitchen junk drawer, found the flashlight and made her way to the closet in the hallway where she'd seen the breaker box. Two of the switches had tripped and she flicked them back to the on position. A small spark made her jump, but the lights did not come back on.

"Crap." She jerked her cell phone from the pocket of her robe, hit Anson's number and started speaking as soon as he answered. "The electricity went out. Does this happen often?"

"I'm driving home now, but all the houses I'm passing have porch lights on."

"I think it's only my house. Two breakers were tripped, but when I flipped them back on nothing happened, except a little spark."

"A spark!" His voice held a note of panic. "Is there smoke? Are you still beside the breaker box?"

"No smoke. I'm right in front of it." She moved the beam of her light all around the metal box just to make sure.

"I'm just around the corner. Don't take your eyes off of it, and if you see or smell anything grab Hannah and get out of the house."

"Now you're scaring me. I was just calling to see if this happens often and you had a trick for fixing it."

The roar of his diesel truck announced his arrival. "I'm here. I'm coming in." The phone line went dead. He didn't knock, just used his key. "Tess?"

"Right here." She waved the flashlight, the beam of the light signaling her location in the hallway.

The heat of his body enveloped her as he pressed close to look over her shoulder. Another kind of spark instantly kindled at her core. "I'm afraid to touch it again."

"I'm glad you didn't," he said. "I'll call the electrician tomorrow. It's probably time to get the old wiring replaced."

"But I need electricity in case Hannah needs a breathing treatment in the night."

"You'll come home with me. You and Hannah can stay with us for as long as you need."

"Will Nan be okay with that?"

"You know she will. Go pack what you need for the night and we can come back for the rest tomorrow in the daylight. I'm going to inspect this box a bit more."

She quickly threw a few items into a duffel bag, then followed Anson into her daughter's room. He scooped Hannah up and cuddled her against one shoulder.

Hannah opened her eyes and smiled. "My chief."

"Go back to sleep, little one. I've got you."

Tess tucked her daughter's favorite blankie around her and pressed a lingering kiss on Anson's lips, her heart fluttering behind her rib cage.

The rain had stopped, and the night air was cold and damp as they walked next door. Anson went straight up the stairs to one of the guest rooms. Tess pulled back the covers and he settled Hannah onto the mattress.

She tucked the blanket under her daughter's chin, kissed her forehead, both cheeks and the tip of her nose. "Sweet dreams, beautiful girl."

He took her hand as they walked from the room, his sly grin hinting at what he wanted to do next.

"Your grandmother might find it inappropriate for us to sleep together under her roof and make you stay downstairs where she can keep an eye on your virtue." Tess knew this wasn't true, but it was fun to tease him.

He chuckled softly and pulled her into a hug. "She knows I'm already ruined. Let's go downstairs and see if she's awake and tell her what's going on."

They found her in bed watching an old black-and-white movie. "Hey, Nan. You're up late," he said.

"I heard you come in and thought there was more than one set of feet going up the stairs."

Tess sat on the foot of her bed. "Sorry we woke you. The electricity is out at my house."

"We'll have company for a while." Anson put a hand on Tess's shoulder. "I'm going to get an electrician to check out the old wiring in my house. I'll probably need to have the whole thing rewired for safety. And until then, Tess and Hannah are going to be staying with us."

"Of course." The wrinkles around her eyes and mouth deepened with her smile. "Make yourself at home, dear."

"Thank you. I'll make sure we aren't too much bother."

"It will be an absolute pleasure to have a house full of people once again."

"Guess I'm boring," Anson said.

"You're not boring. It will just be nice to have a little one running around this big old house. It'll remind me of my own children and grandchildren when they were young." She smiled sweetly, but mischief and scheming gleamed in her eyes. "Anson was the rowdiest one of the whole bunch."

Tess wrapped an arm around his waist. "I would love to hear tales of his childhood mischief."

"I see how it's going to be. The two of you ladies ganging up on me."

"I'll tell you the first story over breakfast," Nan said. "It's late. You two go get some rest."

They rose and bid her good-night. Back upstairs, they stopped in front of the room where Hannah slept.

"Anson, I can't leave Hannah to sleep alone. I'm worried she'll wake up and not know where she is."

"I understand, but it's going to be even harder to have you this close and not in my bed."

She untucked his uniform shirt and slid her palms across his flat stomach then up to tease his nipples. "I suppose I could come for a quick visit."

He shivered and moaned. "I like the way you think, honey."

The next morning, Anson propped his back against the doorframe and admired Tess as she washed breakfast dishes, hips swaying to the song playing on the kitchen radio. "Is there anything special you want to do for your birthday on Friday?"

She glanced over her shoulder with narrowed eyes. "How'd you know it's my birthday? Have you been using your detective skills?"

"Full FBI background check."

She dropped the sponge and spun around. "What?"

"Kidding." He chuckled, then crossed the room and braced his hands on each side of her hips, trapping her against the counter. "Your birth date is on the lease for the house."

"Oh yeah." She slid her still-damp hands into his back pockets. "I don't have anything special in mind."

"I'll see what I can come up with." The feel of her hands on his butt made him want to rush her upstairs before he left for work. "I'd like to take you on a real date soon. Just the two of us."

"I can get behind that plan."

Jenny came into the kitchen and they pulled apart.

"Good morning," the young woman said. "Sorry I'm late."

"No worries." He kissed Tess and paused long enough to inhale her sweet apple scent. "I'm off to work, ladies."

"Stay safe," Tess called after him.

He glanced back and winked. "Always."

Hannah met him at the door, and he scooped her up, tossed her into the air, then set her on her feet. "Have a good day, little one."

"Bye-bye." She turned and ran toward the back of the house.

Waking up with Tess and Hannah under the same roof was something he could get used to. He fought it, but he was starting to hope more and more that she would consider staying in Oak Hollow, because…

I'm in love with Tess Harper.

He'd plunged into uncharted depths. A love deeper than any he'd ever known.

Chapter Fourteen

Tess drifted into awareness when a kiss brushed softly over her lips. Anson's cedarwood aftershave and Hannah's sweet giggle pulled her from the last remnants of sleep, and she opened her eyes. Three faces smiled from behind the flickering glow of birthday candles in the early morning light. A chorus of Happy Birthday brought joyful tears to her eyes.

Hannah wiggled from Anson's arms and bounced on the bed beside her mother. "Blow, Momma."

"And make a wish," Anson added.

Nan stepped closer and held out the cake.

Tess put an arm around her daughter and made the same birthday wish she'd been making since her baby's birth. *Please keep her safe during her sur-*

gery and let it be a success. "This is a wonderful surprise. Thank you."

"It's a tradition in our family," Nan said. "I always woke my children up this way on their birthday."

They were including her in family traditions. And making her want things she shouldn't.

"Hannah, will you please help me take the cake to the kitchen? Your momma and Anson can meet us there in a few minutes."

Once they'd left, Anson reached for something he'd tucked under the bed and handed her a wrapped box. "Happy birthday, honey."

She ripped off the paper and gasped when she saw the purple velvet box from the estate sale. "Is this what I think it is?"

"Open it and find out."

The old hinges creaked. Tears stung the backs of her eyes and tightened her throat. The white gold and aquamarine necklace gleamed up at her, then blurred through happy tears. "Oh, Anson." She placed the open box on the bed beside her and threw her arms around his neck. "I love it. How did you manage to get it?"

"I have my connections." He glanced over his shoulder, then tumbled her onto the bed and kissed her. "Jenny is willing to babysit, if you'd like to join me on a proper date tonight?"

"That sounds great." Her heart was overflowing. "We better go downstairs before Hannah comes back to get us."

They ate cake for breakfast, and Tess enjoyed a beautiful day with her child and the special new people in their lives.

Tess's days and nights in the Curry family's big white house drifted by in a state of contentment. Her usual anxiety began melting away during days spent doing a job she enjoyed and being a mother to her precious girl. And, despite trying to shield her heart, indulging in nights with a man who rocked her world.

A couple of days before Thanksgiving, Tess was sweeping Nan's large front porch when a white Cadillac pulled into the driveway. This older couple had to be Anson's parents. She set the broom aside, went down the steps and waved as they got out of the car.

A pretty woman with brown hair shot through with silver returned her smile. "You must be Tess. We've heard so much about you. I'm Ann, and this is Anson's dad, Mark."

He stuck out a hand and shook hers. "Nice to meet you, young lady."

"I'm happy to meet both of you. Let me help you with your suitcases."

Before they could get to the door, a Suburban pulled up to the curb in front of the house.

"Oh good," Ann said. "Carol and her family are early."

Tess was introduced to Anson's sister, her husband Thomas, and their adorable toddler, Landon. The ring of happy voices drew everyone from inside the house. Watching the Curry family hugging and reconnecting tugged extra hard at her heart and increased her desire to become a member.

In a matter of minutes, the Curry home was bursting with love and laughter. Anytime anxieties about getting too close and being hurt slipped out of her vault of fears, she tucked them away for later consideration. Tess was determined to enjoy the kind of family holiday she hadn't had since childhood.

And something her daughter had never experienced.

When bath time rolled around that first night, Tess went into the family room and discovered Anson asleep in the recliner, with his arms protectively curled around Hannah on one side and Landon on the other. *A Charlie Brown Thanksgiving* played on the big screen TV, holding the attention of the children. She couldn't bring herself to upset the scene and instead sat on the couch and pulled out her phone to take their picture.

I want this in my life. I want this for my child.

On the day before Thanksgiving, Tess answered the front door and found a curvy blonde standing on the welcome mat holding a pie and wearing a startled expression. "Good afternoon."

"Oh, hello." The woman glanced next door at the Craftsman house then back to Tess. "Is Anson here?" She shifted the pie to one hand and tugged at the short hem of her skirt with the other.

"He went to the grocery store for his grandmother." She was determined to be polite, even though she knew the other woman was one of Anson's admirers. "Please, come inside."

"That's okay. I need to get going. I just wanted to drop off this chocolate pie. It's one of his favorites, and I promised I'd bake it for him." She shoved it into Tess's hands and turned to go down the front steps, but stopped before Tess could close the door. "Just tell him I came by and... Well, he knows where to find me."

The grin she flashed made Tess want to throw the pie in her face, and she used her foot to close the front door.

"Who was that?" asked Anson's sister, Carol.

"One of your brother's admiring females. She didn't even tell me her name." She raised the pie and made a face at it. "She brought this chocolate pie she baked just for him and is probably hoping he'll come over and thank her."

Carol let out a quick laugh. "My brother has been a female magnet since he hit puberty." She took the pie from Tess, maybe recognizing her desire to drop it in the nearest trash can. "Don't let her bother you. I see the way he looks at you, like he always wants to kiss you." She turned toward the kitchen and left Tess to stew in her jealousy in the foyer.

She picked up Hannah's little black boots that had been tossed askew after playing outside. The tiny shoes lined up beside a large pair of Anson's boots created a picture that made her breath catch.

She was still standing there daydreaming about a possible future when Anson walked through the front door.

"I got the… What's wrong?"

She put on her best *I'm fine* smile. "Nothing's wrong."

He put the groceries on the entry table and stroked her cheek with a thumb. "I know that's not completely true because your pretty mouth is pinched tight. Think I need to find a secluded spot and soften it up a bit."

Her real smile returned. "How about a quick preview of what's to come for now?"

"I can do that." He closed the distance between them and teased her lips with his own.

"Told you so," Carol said on a laugh as she passed by on her way up the stairs.

He watched his sister with a raised brow. "What's she talking about?"

"She said you'd be back soon." She wasn't about to tell him exactly what Carol had said. "Let's put these groceries away."

He followed her into the kitchen and set the bag on the counter. "Where'd this pie come from?"

She followed his line of sight to the offending chocolate pie. "A gift from one of the members of your 'Pantie Posse.'"

He shot her a startled look, then turned to unload

groceries. "You know about that? It's just something silly my dispatcher made up."

"I've known about it since the day Hannah and I brought cookies to the station. I overheard Betty say something about me being a new member."

"Is that what made you leave in such a hurry that day?"

"Absolutely. I didn't, and still don't, want to be lumped in with that particular club."

He glanced around to see if they were alone, then pulled her into his arms. "Are you jealous, Tess Harper?"

"Of course not." His smirk told her he didn't believe her claim. "Maybe only a teeny, tiny bit jealous. The woman who brought the pie said you'd know where to find her. I think she wants you to thank her in person. And I think we both know what she has in mind."

"Did she say her name?"

She smacked him on the arm. "Oh my God. You don't even know which blonde bimbo made you a chocolate pie?"

"Well, now that I know she's blonde, that narrows the list." He laughed and dodged her next playful punch.

"You're terrible, Anson Curry." She turned to see Nan standing in the doorway with a big grin on her pretty, weathered face.

"You two look like you're having fun." She crossed to the half-unloaded bag of groceries and continued the job Anson had started. "What did I miss during my nap?"

"Someone brought over a homemade chocolate pie for your grandson. Said it was his favorite."

"Pish posh," Nan said. "His favorite is pecan. In fact, that's what we need to make next. Anson, go get Hannah and see if she wants to help me bake."

"Yes, ma'am." He winked at Tess and left the room.

"It makes me very happy to see you and my grandson having fun together. He hasn't been this happy in a long time."

"Truly?"

"Yes. We like having the two of you here with us. I hope you'll give some serious thoughts to staying in Oak Hollow."

Tess almost admitted aloud how much she'd been thinking about it, but Hannah ran into the kitchen.

"I cook, Momma?"

"Yes. Nan would like for you to help her bake Anson's favorite pecan pie."

They gathered all of the ingredients and began mixing, baking and laughing. More family members trickled in and either helped or grabbed a snack.

Landon toddled around the kitchen island yelling his new favorite word. "Daddy, Daddy, Daddy."

Thomas scooped him up and tickled his tummy. "What is it, my little daddy's boy?" He didn't get an answer, just a sloppy kiss.

Tess watched her daughter's eyes following the father and son duo as they left the kitchen.

"The oven is ready for the pies," Nan said.

Hannah ran a finger around the rim of a pie plate. "Circle."

"Is it the circle you've been looking for?" Anson asked.

"No. Not it."

He rubbed a hand across his jaw. "We'll just have to keep looking until we find your circle, little one."

Thanksgiving Day arrived cold and overcast, but the mood inside the Curry home was warm—all were filled with delicious food and overflowing with love. Luckily, the kitchen was big, because it was a hive of cooking activity and much laughter. Hannah and baby Landon had become fast friends, and she followed him around like a little mother, making sure he didn't get into trouble. A few more relatives arrived midmorning, and twelve people sat around the large dining room table to share the meal.

Tess fought happy tears for the beautiful day she and her daughter enjoyed with this wonderful family. Sad tears that it was temporary. Worried tears because Hannah would definitely take it hard when they left for their next home in Houston. They were only visitors, not members of the family.

But could we be? Can I take the risk that he really wants a life with us? And won't change his mind?

Was it possible they could come back to Oak Hollow and make a forever home in this small town after Hannah was released from the hospital? Her heart screamed for her to do exactly that.

After dessert, Tess joined Anson and the kids in the sunroom.

"I'll see you when you get here." Anson slid his phone into his pocket, then put the wooden train back on the track and pushed it over to Landon. "Hannah, remember when we talked about how the puppy will be my pet, but you can be his friend?"

"Yes." She climbed onto her knees and patted his chest. "You puppy."

"That's right. And I have exciting news."

Tess sat on the floor across from them. Her little girl's wide-eyed gaze was locked on Anson's face.

"The puppy is coming home today," he said.

Her little mouth snapped into an O, and she threw her arms around his neck. "Puppy! I wuv you, Daddy."

Tess froze as tingling goose bumps sprang to life on her skin, and she exhaled a shaky breath. Maybe she'd called him Daddy because Landon had been calling his own father that incessantly. Maybe it was an innocent mistake.

Or maybe Hannah had fallen in love with him, just like she had.

An overwhelming fear that Anson would suddenly stop wanting them slammed into her heart. Would both her and her daughter be hurt because she'd been too weak to resist falling for Anson? She quickly excused herself and hurried upstairs to the bedroom she'd been sharing with Anson after Hannah fell asleep each night.

Anson slipped into the room a few minutes later, closed the door and turned on the CD player. "Dance with me, honey."

She stopped pacing and stared at him. "She called you Daddy."

"I know."

"We need to talk to her, but I have no idea what to say. I can't tell her about her real father or why he…didn't want her." The last words came out in a strangled whisper and her gut cramped.

He pulled her into his arms, tucked her head under his chin and swayed to the music. "Has she never asked about her father?"

"No, and I've always dreaded the day she does. Do I make something up? Tell her he died? Do I lie to my daughter to save her feelings? She's too young to understand."

"Maybe you can wait on this conversation." He stroked her back as he spoke. "I bet she only said it because Landon says it constantly. She may not even realize what she called me."

"I had the same thought. I'm worried she just wants to be like other kids with two parents. I need to remind her that we're…leaving."

He stopped swaying and tilted her face up to meet his gaze. "I think you and I should talk about Houston."

"What about it?"

"You could stay here. With me."

She tensed and babbled incoherent sounds. He seemed to be sharing her dangerous thoughts, but before she could say a word, he brushed a finger over her lips.

"Don't answer that, yet. Let's enjoy the holiday together, see what else Hannah says and take some time to settle into the idea. There's no rush."

The tip of her tongue flicked out to moisten her lower lip. "Okay." Flutters danced in her belly, teasing her with possibilities.

The doorbell rang, and Anson kissed her forehead. "That should be my friend with the puppy. Let's go make Hannah smile."

The adorable little animal caused major excitement and a ton of laughter as he scampered around on three good legs and sniffed everyone.

"What should we name him?" Anson asked Hannah.

She lay on her belly nose to nose with the puppy and giggled when he licked her face. "Puppy name Sheriff."

Tess shared a smile with Anson before he settled on the floor beside her daughter.

"That's a perfect name, Little One."

Once both small children were tucked into bed and Sheriff slept in his doggie crate, the adults relaxed in the living room with cups of hot cider spiked with a bit of spiced rum. While his little sister told a story about her toddler's first time at the zoo, Anson slid his arm around Tess's shoulders and tugged her tighter against his side. Her smile was sweet, and it made him want to carry her off to some secret place and keep her naked all night long.

"Anson? Did you hear me, son?" His mother said.

"No. Sorry. What did you say?"

His little sister stifled a laugh behind her hand and then tried to cover it with a cough. He playfully nudged her foot with his.

"Do you have the day off tomorrow?" his mother repeated.

"I work the early shift. Why?"

"Son, what do we always do on that day?"

"Get a Christmas tree," Anson said. "I can go midafternoon, if everyone is willing to wait for me."

"We'll wait for you." Nan pushed herself up to stand. "I'm ready to get my beauty sleep. Tomorrow will be another busy day." As she walked past Tess, she patted her shoulder. "I'm glad you're here with us."

Tess reached up to squeeze her hand. "You have an amazing family. Sleep well."

Carol, wearing her playful smile, stood and tugged on her husband's arm. "We're headed to bed as well. Our little boy always wakes up bright and early."

"Good night, everyone," Thomas said, and gave Anson a fist bump on the way by.

His mother gathered up empty mugs. "Guess I'll do the same. You two should enjoy the fire until it burns down a bit, but make sure it's out before you go to bed."

"Yes, ma'am." He loved his family, and always enjoyed their big gatherings, but it was nice to be alone with Tess.

She cuddled against his side and hooked one leg over his knee. "My family also used to put the tree up right after Thanksgiving. Christmas is my favorite season."

"You consider it a whole season?" He shivered when her fingers trailed back and forth along his forearm.

"Absolutely. It's the season that encompasses the end of fall through the start of winter."

"So, your seasons are summer, fall, Christmas, winter and spring?"

"That's right. Please tell me you aren't one of those grinchy people?"

He laughed and pulled her hand up to kiss her palm. "No. I love it. It's my favorite holiday. I mean *season*."

She wiped a hand across her brow in an overdramatized show of relief. "Thank goodness."

This woman is adorable. "I did notice about eight boxes marked Xmas when I helped you move in."

"I don't have a lot of possessions, but my decorations are very important to me. Some of the ornaments belonged to my grandparents."

"You don't have more furniture and stuff in storage somewhere?"

"No. After my divorce I had very little. My first apartment after I left Brent was furnished. I bought cheap stuff along the way but sold most of it before we came to Texas." She sighed.

"What's wrong, honey?"

"I was planning to do Christmas up really big this year for Hannah. Get a real tree. Hang stockings by our first fireplace. I had all kinds of plans for how I wanted to decorate the Craftsman house, but it doesn't look like the wiring will be finished anytime soon."

He tipped her chin up and kissed her lips. "I'm sorry about that. Tomorrow we'll buy a second tree and you can put your Christmas stuff in the formal living room."

Joy brightened her eyes. "You think Nan will be okay with that?"

"Of course she will." He bit his lip to keep himself from once again bringing up the topic of her staying in Oak Hollow. Permanently.

The following evening, everyone decorated the big tree in the family room. After that, Tess, Hannah and Anson worked on the second tree in the formal living room. A Bing Crosby Christmas album played, and she told her daughter about each ornament's history as they hung them on the tree.

"This star belonged to my parents," she said. "They bought it on their first Christmas together."

"Star," Hannah cheered. "It make Christmas safe?"

"I think it will, sweetie. Let me hold you up and you can put it on the top of the tree."

Her sweet girl held the star with both hands as she lifted her up. Anson came around beside them to help her slide it onto the top branch, then they stood back to admire their work. The ornaments glistened and the lights glowed softly with all the colors of Christmas.

He wrapped his arms around them and kissed their cheeks. "Beautiful."

Chapter Fifteen

Tess hung up the phone after confirming Hannah's cardiologist appointment. It was the checkup where they'd run final tests before the January surgery. The day was growing closer, and there was nothing she could do to stop it. Not knowing how Hannah's recovery would be, she hadn't accepted any of the offered jobs. Thank goodness for the divorce settlement money. She bit her fingernail and leaned on the railing of the back porch as the sun dipped lower in the sky.

Anson came up behind her, wrapped his arms around her waist and kissed the top of her head. "You look like you have the weight of the world on your back."

She allowed herself to lean against him and soak up his comfort. "I just confirmed Hannah's appointment in Houston."

"Are you sure you don't want me to go with you?"

"No need. It's just a few noninvasive tests and a chat with the doctor. I know you have that meeting with the city council."

"Come take a walk with me. You can tell me what's on your mind."

"A walk sounds nice." Tess checked on Hannah, then they put on their coats. She accepted his hand and laced their fingers.

Dried leaves swirled around and crunched under their feet. The first Christmas lights were appearing on some of the houses, and the scent of wood fires filled the evening air. Neither of them spoke for a few minutes, and she let the beautiful moment wrap around her. "I've been thinking about what's next for me and Hannah. When we're in Houston, I'm also supposed to check out apartments. But…"

He stopped walking and pulled her hand to his lips. "What are you trying to tell me, honey?"

She rested her head on her favorite spot on his chest, and her tension eased when he wrapped his arms around her. "I've been considering *not* staying in Houston."

"Please tell me you're staying in Oak Hollow."

Houston was a huge city that held opportunities, but it didn't hold any appeal for her as a long-term home. The appeal was in the man with his arms wrapped around her, the family that filled his home and the town that she'd grown to love. His tight embrace gave her the courage to say the words aloud. "I'm giving it some serious consideration."

A smile spread across his handsome face. "That makes me very happy."

In the hospital waiting room, Hannah played blocks alongside a little boy, and he asked her where her mother was.

"My Momma." She pointed at Tess and smiled her most adorable smile.

A smile that filled her with love and thankfulness that God had entrusted this amazing little girl to her.

"Where is your daddy?" the other child said.

Tess flinched and braced for Hannah's answer.

"My Daddy home. He chief." Hannah ran over and climbed onto her lap. "Momma, when we go home?"

"Tomorrow. We're spending one night in a hotel."

"I want my home. My Daddy. My Nan."

Me, too. The feelings that rushed in brought tears to her eyes. She'd been asking the universe for a sign of what to do. Her daughter's matter-of-fact statement felt like the answer she'd been seeking. They should stay in Oak Hollow with the people they had fallen in love with. She almost pulled out her phone to call Anson and tell him she'd made her decision, but a nurse stepped out and called Hannah's name.

After Hannah had her EKG and echocardiogram they sat across from the cardiologist in his office.

Tess could tell by the look on his face that the news was not good.

"We need to move up the date of Hannah's surgery. I'd like to schedule it for a week from today."

Tess's heart stumbled painfully in her chest.

She thought about driving straight back to Oak Hollow, to the comfort of Anson's arms. But she was mentally and physically exhausted. She got Hannah something to eat but couldn't stomach anything herself. They checked into their hotel and Hannah was asleep ten minutes after her bath and story time. Tess continued to hold her in her arms long after she had drifted into dreamland.

She had planned to make this Christmas as wonderful and magical as possible for Hannah, and deal with the surgery and recovery after that. But now the holiday plans she had made would be interrupted and cut short.

I'm not ready yet!

The following morning, Tess couldn't wait to get out of the chaotic city and back to the soothing Hill Country landscape. They arrived in Oak Hollow just before lunch, and she drove through the town square to see if Anson was free to join them for a meal at the Acorn. She found a parking spot, got Hannah out of her seat and hurried inside. A crowd of people filled the usually calm police station.

Her nerves—already frayed from the surgery

change—unraveled a bit more. She hoped to see Anson sitting behind his big desk, but he wasn't anywhere in sight within the flurry of activity. The rush of movement, worried faces and raised voices were all signs that something was wrong.

Before she could ask anyone what was happening, she heard Walker's voice come over Betty's radio.

"Officer down. Officer down. We need an ambulance to the Seaton place."

The blood seemed to crystallize in her veins, and she squeezed Hannah tighter against her chest. It wasn't Anson's voice over the radio, which meant…

Anson! No!

An ugly wave of fear slammed into her and swelled painfully behind her rib cage. She clung to Hannah and stood frozen in place while everyone rushed around them. At the moment she wasn't even sure how to take her next breath. The possibility of losing him in the line of duty was one of her fears coming to life. The main reason she'd resisted a relationship with Anson. Why hadn't she listened to her gut and kept her distance? Why had she allowed her daughter to get close enough to love him?

I can't go through this again. I can't bear to see another flag pulled off a coffin and folded into a triangle.

Memories of receiving news about her father and brother rushed in with a vicious strike. Her plans to stay in Oak Hollow, stay with Anson, suddenly seemed like the worst idea in the world. Hannah whimpered and buried her face against her neck. Tess held her a little tighter and moved closer to Betty to see what she could hear.

"What's happened?" she called out to anyone who would listen.

One of the officers' wives stepped up beside her. "A meth lab was discovered on the outskirts of town."

"Is Chief Curry there?" *Please say no.*

"Yes. He was first on the scene with Officer Walker."

"Is he..." Tess couldn't finish the question.

"That's all I know."

Nausea rolled in her gut and she clapped a hand to her mouth. She ran for the bathroom, and barely made it in time to set Hannah on her feet and throw up in the toilet.

Hannah stood behind her and patted her back. "Momma owie."

She didn't know what to think or do or feel, but she had to get her daughter out of this chaos. But first she had to spend a few more minutes with her face hovering over a nasty public toilet. After there was nothing left in her stomach, she splashed water on her face, looked at herself in the mirror and took a deep breath. She needed to find out what had happened, but at the same time, she was scared to find out. She could just keep her fingers crossed that he was fine.

"Momma, where my Daddy?"

She gripped the edge of the sink tighter. "I'm not sure, sweetie." *Stop being a chicken. Stop putting it off.*

She needed to get Hannah out of here and... *Nan.* She had to get to Nan in case she'd heard about this and was upset. What if she was alone?

"Sweetie, wrap your arms and legs around me and hold on tight." She kissed her baby's cheek and resisted the urge to cry as they rushed through the chaos of the small station. Her pulse raced and her hands trembled so badly she couldn't manage to start the car. She let her head drop to the top of the steering wheel.

"Momma?"

"It's okay, sweetie. I'm just tired from driving so far this morning." She probably shouldn't be driving, even the few blocks home, but she'd go slowly. Nan had a reputation for knowing things before anyone else. Maybe she already knew something, because she couldn't bear to receive life-shattering news in public with Hannah.

Mary Grant's car was out front. Tess got Hannah out of her booster seat, and they rushed inside the house.

"Nan, where are you?"

"In the kitchen," she called out.

Hannah ran ahead, and she followed to find Nan and Mary standing at the butcher block island.

Mary's husband, Victor, held a cell phone to his ear. "Thank you. That's great news."

Tess's heart fluttered with hope.

"Anson is okay. He's at the hospital now."

"Let's go," Tess and Nan said in unison.

Victor held up a hand. "The paramedic is my nephew, and he said Anson wants everyone to wait here." The older man took a step back when all three women started talking at once. "Ladies, he's okay. Just a little banged up. He'll be home soon."

"But surely he can't drive himself," Tess said.

"Walker will drive him."

Hannah came out of the pantry with a bag of chocolate chips. "Cookies. For my Daddy."

Mary knelt before her. "Can I help you make the cookies?"

The little girl nodded eagerly.

Tess was extremely grateful Mary was helping her with Hannah. The two of them disappeared back into the butler's pantry.

"I don't want to sit at home and worry," Nan complained. "I should be there with my grandson."

Victor took her hand and encouraged her to take a seat. "He worries about you. If you go to the hospital, it will just make him more stressed. You know he's in good hands, and they'll have him back to you in no time."

"He's really okay?" Tess interrupted, and stood behind Nan with one hand on her shoulder.

"He's going to be just fine. I'm going to start a pot of coffee." He walked away and gave the two of them a moment alone.

"Tess, dear, what do you think we should do?"

She sat beside the frightened grandmother. Another stroke might... She had to keep Nan calm. "I was so incredibly scared when I heard. I still am. Rushing to him is my first instinct, but I guess we should do what he has asked."

Nan shook her head. "Why do some people insist on doing dangerous jobs?"

"I wonder the same thing." *I don't think I can do this.* The panic was rising once again. She kept her tone low so Hannah wouldn't hear. "I promised myself long ago that I would never love a man that was in the military or a cop or a firefighter or any of those jobs."

The older woman's hands found both of hers. "Do you love my grandson?"

Tears brimmed in her eyes, but she blinked them away. "That doesn't matter. I'm a mother, and Hannah must be my first priority. Maybe she should be my only priority."

"You can't spend your life alone. And it's a whole lot easier to raise a child with a partner. Don't let this scare ruin what could become a beautiful family."

"This scare has reminded me of how things can end."

"It doesn't have to."

"I watched my mother go through it with my father when I was little. He was a cop in San Diego and was shot and killed. Then my big brother died overseas in the Navy when I was eighteen. It killed her, literally. She found out right after my brother's death that she had cancer, but she didn't tell me. And she decided not to get any treatment and let herself die. I was left all alone in the world."

"My sweet girl, I know life can be scary. And I know what it is to lose someone you love, but you can't shut life out. Don't let it beat you. Learn from your mother and don't repeat her mistakes."

"But I have to think of Hannah." They both looked at the little girl standing on a step stool pouring a cup of sugar into a mixing bowl.

"I understand, but please think about what I've said. Look at how happy she is at this moment. Don't make any hasty decisions."

Tess excused herself from the kitchen, ran upstairs to Anson's room, sat on his bed and let herself have a moment to cry.

Anson wanted Walker to leave him at the end of the sidewalk after driving him home from the hospital, but his friend and coworker insisted on getting him all the way into the house. He limped through the front door with multiple contusions, his arm in a sling and stitches behind one ear. All he wanted was to hug his grandmother and his little one, and wrap his arms tight around Tess and inhale her scent. And know that he was alive.

The explosion at the meth lab had slammed him against the side of a building and knocked him out cold. He'd woken to sounds and smells that caused flashbacks of his time in the Marines, soon followed by pain radiating through his body. It had been scary as hell.

"I'm home."

Tess appeared in the foyer within seconds, but stood like a statue; only her wide, frantic eyes moved as she scanned his form from top to bottom. Then she rushed forward and launched herself at him, pulling back just enough not to hurt him, not too badly. Her hands touched him everywhere, gently probing and finding newly forming bruises and making him grit his teeth to keep from letting her know.

"Where are you hurt? What happened to you? Should you really be out of the hospital yet?"

He started to answer one of her many questions, but her mouth was pressed hard against his. He put his one free arm around her and breathed in her sweet apple scent. "I'm okay, honey." He glanced up and saw Hannah and Nan staring at them. "I'm okay," he repeated.

Hannah bounced up and down at his feet and raised her arms. "Up, pease."

"He can't pick you up right now, sweetie," Tess said.

His little one stood on his most injured side with his bound arm. He wanted to scream because he couldn't swing her up into the air like he often did. Tess met his gaze, and no doubt knowing his thoughts, she picked up her daughter and nestled her between them.

"You got owie?" Her tiny hands patted his cheeks.

"Just a few, little one. I'll be all better real soon."

Nan dabbed her eye with a tissue, and Tess stepped back so she could hug him. He cursed the damn sling that kept him from wrapping both of his arms tight around all three of them.

Walker cleared his throat and held out a bag. "Here are his meds and stuff."

"What's in there?" she asked.

Anson tried to grab it, but Tess got to it first, opened the paper bag and dumped it onto the entry table. She shook a bottle of pills, then read the label. "Pain medication. What is this ointment for?"

"His stitches," Walker added unhelpfully.

Anson shot him a pointed look that said "Thanks for not having my back."

"Stitches? Where?" Tess dropped the items back onto the table and started poking and prodding him again.

"Behind my left ear," he said before she accidentally touched it, but her attention brought a small smile to his face. "It's only three stitches."

"Let's get him into bed," Nan suggested to Tess.

"I'm right here," Anson said. "And I don't want to get in bed. I'll just sit for a bit in the recliner. And you can both stop fussing over me." Truthfully, he didn't want to be alone in his bedroom to relive the accident. He needed to be surrounded by activity and the people he loved.

Tess snapped her hands to her hips. "Not fuss?

Seriously? Do you have any idea how scared we all were? If you weren't hurt, I would spank you, Anson Curry."

"Oh no," Hannah said, and put a little hand over her mouth.

Walker turned and laughed into his fist. When he still couldn't contain himself, he stepped outside, his deep laugh drifting in through the closed door.

Anson shook his head, walked past the ladies and eased into the leather recliner in the living room. He really wanted a pain pill, but didn't want to ask for one and admit how much he was hurting.

A moment later, Tess appeared at his side with a glass of water and pill in her hand. "Take this."

"Thanks." He popped it into his mouth and downed half of the glass of water.

She sat on the stuffed arm of the recliner and stroked his cheek. "If I didn't already say so, I'm really glad you're okay."

"Cookies." Hannah presented a plate with three fresh from the oven, homemade cookies.

"Thank you. Did you bake these for me, little one?"

"Yes. I bake."

He took a big bite. Warm, sweet chocolate melted on his tongue. "So good."

"Milk," Hannah said, and ran back toward the kitchen.

Tess snatched one of his cookies.

"Hey, those are mine," he joked.

"Well, I'm starving. I've been throwing up everything I eat for days."

He put down his half-eaten treat and studied her. "You got sick?"

"No. I got scared."

Luckily she was sitting on the side with his unbound arm, and he wrapped it around her waist. "I'm sorry, honey."

Hannah returned with a glass of milk, put it on the small side table and took the third cookie from his plate.

"Why is everyone stealing my cookies?"

Hannah giggled and pointed at Nan, who was walking into the room with another plate. And she was moving just like her old perky self. He got his wish of being in the middle of everything. But he couldn't miss the way Tess watched her daughter's every move, and her eyes were filled with sadness.

And what looked like... Fear.

His chest tightened and his alert went up. Something was wrong. He'd talked to her on the phone the night before, and she'd said everything was fine and she'd tell him about the cardiologist appointment when they got home. But she hadn't said a word. He was done waiting and would ask her once the little one was asleep. They kept him entertained until Tess took Hannah upstairs for her bath.

Nan sat down beside him. "Are you really okay?"

"Just sore, and I want to take this sling off. Thank God my arm isn't broken. Dr. Clark said I can take it off as soon as my shoulder moves without pain. What about you? I hate putting stress on you."

"I'm tougher than you think. But you need to talk to Tess. She's mighty spooked by what happened today. She told me about her father and brother. And then her poor mother."

He gently touched the bandage over his stitches that were already starting to itch. "I was afraid of this. How do I make her feel safe?"

"All you can do is tell her about the life you want with her and Hannah. Just speak from your heart. Don't hold back. Tell her how much you love her."

He raised his brows. "So, you can tell?"

She chuckled. "Of course I can."

"And you don't think it's crazy that I'm already in love with her?"

She glanced at her wedding portrait on the wall. "I fell in love with your grandfather on the very day we met. But I made him work for it before I told him. There's no timeline when the heart is involved."

"Thanks for the advice. I'm going upstairs." He took his time getting out of the recliner. "Are you okay for the evening? Because I probably won't come back down unless you need me."

"I'm just fine. I'm going to get into bed and read for a bit."

Tess sat on the side of the tub while Hannah swirled her toy mermaid through the bubbles. Her skin and nerves felt raw, her heart too exposed to the sensations of the world. The memories of being told about her father's then her brother's deaths replayed on a loop. They'd both been tragically and unexpectedly taken, but her mother had chosen to leave her behind. She hadn't been enough for her own mother to fight to live. She hadn't been enough for Hannah's father.

Tess sucked in a sharp breath and drew a shaky hand up to cover her mouth. *I'm not enough. I never have been. And Anson will realize it, too.*

"Momma, I done."

She shook her head and focused on her daughter, barely managing to pull herself out of the near panic. "Pull the stopper, please." She helped her climb out of the tub, wrapped her in a towel, then cuddled her against her chest. "I love you so much, sweet girl."

"Wuv you, Momma."

"Do you want to wear your Wonder Woman nightgown or striped pajamas?"

"Won Woman, pease." Hannah wiggled out of the towel and held up her arms for her mother to slip the nightie over her head. She kissed Tess on the cheek, then opened the bathroom door just as Anson knocked.

"Oh good. I didn't miss story time," he said.

Tess stood to hang up the towel but couldn't meet his eyes.

"You read *Goodnight Moon*." Hannah took him by the hand and they crossed the hall to the bedroom.

She couldn't go in there and share this evening's

bedtime routine like everything was fine. Not now that she realized what had to be done.

She had to leave Oak Hollow…and not come back.

lowed him into his bedroom and standing

Chapter Sixteen

Tess crossed the hall and stuck her head into the bedroom. "Hannah Lynn, would it be okay if Anson reads to you tonight so Momma can take a bath?"

Her daughter tilted her head and crossed her little arms. "Okay."

She spun away and closed herself in the bathroom before anyone could argue. While she soaked in the bath, she listened to the two of them laughing and talking until it grew silent. She quietly slipped into the bedroom dressed in flannel pajamas. Hannah was sound asleep, and he was propped up against the headboard. With a wince of pain, he rose from the bed and motioned for her to follow.

She couldn't put off talking to him, so she followed him into his bedroom and closed the door. He took off his sling and lay down on the bed, but she didn't join him. She crossed to the window and pulled back the curtain to stare at the night sky. If only the stars could grant her wishes and keep everyone she loved safe from harm.

"When I called you in Houston last night, you said you'd tell me about Hannah's appointment when you got home. I can tell something's wrong."

She sat on the foot of the bed and glanced at him from the corner of her eye. "They moved up the surgery."

He sat up, winced and rubbed his shoulder. "Why?"

She knew he was trying to hide his pain, but could see it on his face and in the way he held his body. "The echocardiogram showed enlargement of her heart." Her own heart thumped harder and she rubbed her chest. "I can't talk about it right now."

"Honey, don't shut me out. You can talk to me about anything."

She jumped to her feet and rounded on him, vision blurry with unshed tears. "Until you aren't around to talk to."

"I'm not going anywhere."

His deep voice held a promise she longed to believe. "You can't know that. You can't promise that. Especially with your job."

"Nothing in life is guaranteed." He slowly stood

and reached for her. "Except how I feel about you and Hannah."

Her chest filled with flutters, and she almost took his hand, wanting more than anything to curl up in his arms and cry. Instead, she stumbled back a step. "I don't know how to do this with you. Just when you think everything is great, just when you let your guard down, this is what happens." She motioned to the arm he held across his waist.

He closed the distance between them. "How do you feel about me? Tell me the truth. Hell, at least tell yourself the truth."

Silent screams reverberated in her head. *I love you!* But that truth couldn't be shared. "You know I care about you. That won't change, but I can't give you what you want."

He remained silent and still as a statue, only the pulse throbbing at his throat.

It gutted her to see the stark look of devastation hardening his handsome face. "I don't know how to be what you need and deserve."

"I don't believe you." His tone was measured and deep, but on the verge of shattering.

"Everything I do, every decision I make, every day I get out of bed has to be for Hannah. She has to be my focus. I can't afford to be distracted by romance."

His mouth dropped open. "Distracted? Tess, you can't continue to be the only one in her life. What if you're the one something happens to? Then who will take care of her?"

A new dose of frustrated guilt heaped on top of her worries. She didn't want to acknowledge or think about what he was saying. "I've been taking care of myself since my mother died. I've been taking care of Hannah all by myself since the day she was born." Her voice was rising with each word and tears streamed freely down her cheeks. "Don't you understand? I can't allow myself to need anyone." On the verge of hysteria, she fisted and crossed her hands over her chest.

"Tess—"

"Anson, I can't put another folded flag on my shelf."

He wrapped his good arm around her shoulders, pulled her close and kissed her tear-streaked cheeks. "Honey, please don't cry. Needing and loving people is part of life. Let me hold you tonight, and we can talk tomorrow. Things always look better in the light of day."

As if her arms had a mind of their own, she encircled his waist and surrendered to their connection, pressing her ear to his pounding heart. She'd lose herself in his comfort…one more time. She kissed him like a woman starving.

Not another word was spoken. In slow, careful movements they made love, using touch to share undeclared feelings. Knowing it was the last time, she fell asleep tucked against his body, sheltered in his embrace.

* * *

The glass covering Anson's open coffin was cold and unyielding under her pounding fists, and she couldn't catch her breath. Her throat burned. Her eyes stung. Her heart shattered. No matter how hard she struck the barrier or how loud she screamed, she'd never touch him again. Never feel his heartbeat or his warmth. Never share her life with him.

Tess woke with her pulse racing and sweat coating her skin. Anson moaned in his sleep when she jostled him but remained in a pain medication-induced deep sleep. Moonlight shone in the window, casting him in a ghostly glow, and his chest rose and fell with deep even breaths. It would kill her to ever see his chest stop moving, as it had in the bad dream that awakened her.

Leaving him was her safest option. Her only option.

She eased from under the covers and spent several minutes standing beside the bed, trying her best to memorize everything about him. It was three o'clock in the morning, but she slipped into the bathroom, dressed and then packed what they'd need for a few weeks in Houston. She'd come back—or send for—the rest of their things at a later date.

When everything was loaded into her SUV, she wrote a letter to Nan and one to Anson. Tess tiptoed upstairs to the guest room she'd shared with Hannah and wrapped a thick blanket around her before quietly descending the stairs. At the bottom of the staircase she looked up and almost rushed to him. Instead, she blew a kiss, and her heart shredded in her chest.

I love you, Anson. I'll always love you.

A myriad of aches and pains woke Anson, and he reached for Tess, but her side of the bed was cold and empty. He rubbed sleep and the narcotic haze from his eyes and struggled to sit up. He fumbled with the bottle of pain pills on the nightstand and took one. Tess was probably downstairs feeding Hannah breakfast. And he could definitely use a giant mug of coffee.

When he got to the kitchen, only Nan was there, staring out the breakfast table window. When she turned to him, he saw the tears on her face and rushed forward.

"What's wrong?"

"Sit down, Anson."

He eased onto a chair. "You're scaring me."

"I'm so sorry, but...they left."

The hair stood up on the back of his neck, and his pulse thundered. "What do you mean, they left?"

"She and Hannah left for Houston early this morning. There's a note for each of us." She slid an envelope across the table, then stood. "I'll leave you alone to read it."

His heart thundered, but he felt numb. He stared at the envelope, stark white against the table. After a few agonizing minutes, he slid a finger under the flap and hissed at the sting of a paper cut. "Shit. That figures." He unfolded the paper with a shaking hand.

Anson,
I'm so very sorry I can't be what you need. I can't bear to say goodbye in person, but please know that I'm thankful for everything. I will never forget you or our time together.

He crumpled the note in his fist and clutched it against his heart. "Left for a second time. Seriously?"

Just when he was ready to drink himself into oblivion, even though it was early morning, one thought stopped him. Hannah's surgery. He didn't know the date, and he needed to be there. Maybe his grandmother's letter held more information.

He found her staring out at the garden, no doubt already missing their little one. "Nan, did your note say anything about Hannah's new surgery date?"

"New date? No. I didn't even know it had been changed."

Panic rose up his throat. "I have to get my cell phone."

But she did not answer his call or return any of his messages.

Late that night, Nan came into the kitchen where Anson was brooding at the table with a bottle of whiskey that he should definitely not be mixing with pain pills, but the ache he was feeling was more than narcotics could fix.

"I got it," she said, and waved a piece of paper.

"What?"

"Dr. Clark made a few inquiries and found out Hannah's surgery date."

He took the piece of paper she shook his direction. "December 7 at eight o'clock in the morning."

"If your arm is out of the sling, you can drive us to Houston the day before."

"You're damn right about that."

Hannah jumped on the hotel room bed. "Momma, home, pease."

"We have to stay here a little longer, sweetie." Tess turned away from her daughter so she wouldn't see the tear scalding a streak down her cheek. She stared out at the Houston skyline, and the ache inside her gaped open bigger than Texas. "Remember that apartment we saw yesterday? We'll move into it after the nice doctors make your heart all better."

"No, Momma. Not that. Home." She climbed off the bed and hugged her mother's legs. "I want my Daddy. My Nan."

Tess picked up her child and clutched her tight against her chest, fighting her own desire to return to Oak Hollow. "Sweet girl, I love you so much. It's just you and me again."

They cried together.

Early on the morning of Hannah's surgery, Anson made his way through the hallways of Texas Children's Hospital until he found her room. His pulse thumped double when he caught sight of his girls. Tess was asleep in a recliner, but even in slumber, the strain of the situation etched tension on her beautiful face. He stepped into the room, and Hannah opened her eyes, her expression blooming into a huge smile.

She climbed onto her knees and held up her arms. "You here."

Ignoring his injured shoulder, he lifted her into his arms and splayed his hand across her tiny back, taking a moment to feel her heartbeat.

"Daddy," she whispered, and wrapped her little arms tighter around his neck.

He met Tess's shocked expression over Hannah's head.

"Momma, look." She patted his chest.

"I see, sweetie." Tess climbed to her feet and straightened her hair. "What are you doing here?"

His shoulder was screaming, so he put Hannah back onto the bed. "I needed to be here."

Tess ducked her head. "I'm glad you came...for Hannah. How did you know her surgery is today?"

"Dr. Clark made a few calls." The pain in her eyes almost broke him. He walked around the bed and cradled one side of Tess's face. "I'm here for you, too." The soft slide of her palm over the back of his hand sent a shiver through him.

"I'm sorry about the way I left."

He wrapped his arms around her, and his tension eased when she returned the embrace.

When he winked at her, Hannah smiled, picked up Boo Bunny and rolled over to play.

"I've had time to think and look at things from your perspective," he whispered against Tess's ear. "We've both been fooled by what we thought we were getting in a partner."

"It's not that. It's…"

"My job?"

She nodded and looked up with troubled eyes. "My child *has* to be my focus."

"I know. Nan and Jenny are here, too. They're waiting for me to call them."

She released a deep breath. "That's good."

"I'm here for Hannah. I'll always be there for her. And you and I aren't done either, but we can table that conversation for later. We'll figure things out when Hannah is out of the hospital."

She shook her head and pulled away, leaving his arms empty once again.

"I don't know how to live with the daily fear that…you won't come home from work."

Just as he geared up to argue, a nurse entered the room with paperwork. Now was not the time for this discussion. He'd wait and find the right time to try and ease her fears.

Tess struggled to concentrate on the pages she was signing, while her daughter animatedly talked with her visitors.

Thank goodness they came. Shame washed over

her. How could she have let her fear of heartache prevent her daughter from having the people she needed around her?

A nurse came in to do one of the many things Tess dreaded—putting in an IV. The numbing cream would hopefully do its job and limit the pain of the needle stick.

Hannah sat on her mother's lap with one arm stretched out to the side.

Anson knelt before them and blocked Hannah's view of what the nurse was doing. "I brought something for you." He pulled his chief of police badge from his pocket and pinned it onto her hospital gown.

"Star safe." Hannah's smile beamed, and she put her free hand over the metal badge.

The young nurse looked up from her work. "Oh, she can't—"

Tess stopped her with a shake of her head. She knew his badge couldn't go into the operating room, but Hannah needed the comfort it would give her now.

The nurse gave a nod and finished her task.

Hannah frowned at the IV in her arm but watched in fascination as machines came to life with lights and sounds.

"My sweet girl, this nice nurse is going to give you some medicine. It will make you sleepy." A sharp knot clawed at Tess's throat. "While you are asleep, the doctor will make you all better."

"Okay, Momma."

She pressed her lips to Hannah's forehead, both cheeks and the tip of her nose. "Momma loves you so much, precious girl."

"I wuv you, Momma." She turned her big smile on Anson. "I wuv you, Daddy Chief."

Tess saw a tremor run through him before he leaned forward and pressed his lips to her daughter's forehead.

"I love you, too, little one."

The nurse injected medication into the IV, and within moments, Hannah's beautiful eyes fluttered closed. And Tess almost screamed for her to open them. What if she never saw her baby blues again? "Please take good care of my sweet girl."

"We will. It's time for us to take her back and get started," one of the nurses said, and unlocked the rolling wheels on the bed.

Panic rose with a painful lash, and Tess wanted to scream. She kept a hold of Hannah as they rolled the bed down the hallway, her heart riding painfully up her throat. Anson stayed right beside her.

Be strong. Do not fall apart!

Tess trembled violently when she was forced to let go of her baby's tiny hand and watch them roll the bed through the double doors toward the operating room. Just when she took a step to run after them for one more kiss, Anson's arms wrapped tightly around her.

"I've got you, honey. I'm here, and I'm not going anywhere."

"They've got my life in their hands. My whole world." She clung to him and let the rise and fall of his chest ground her.

They stood locked in their embrace for several minutes as the hustle and bustle of the hospital went on around them. Anson led her into the waiting room, and they took seats near Nan and Jenny.

When she was able to swallow down the knot lodged in her throat, she met everyone's eyes. "Thank you for coming. Even after the way I left."

Nan clasped her hand. "Don't you worry about that. We wouldn't be anywhere else."

The hours ticked by and everyone did their best to keep her occupied, but every minute was an agonizing bit of forever. Finally, the cardiac surgeon, Dr. Fraser, and his surgical nurse were walking toward them. Tess watched as the nurse sighed deeply and folded her hands in front of her. The expression and movement were like a punch to the gut.

Oh my God, no! Something went wrong!

She jumped to her feet, ready to scream, but before she could cry out or beg to know what had happened, Dr. Fraser smiled.

"Everything went beautifully and Hannah is in recovery."

He continued with details, but all Tess could do was wipe away tears of relief and rest her head on Anson's chest.

* * *

The ladies went home the following day. For the next two nights, she and Anson slept on couches in the large ICU waiting room with other scared parents. During those hours, they talked about many things, but they did not discuss their relationship or the future.

Once Hannah was in a private hospital room, Anson needed to return to Oak Hollow for a court date.

As he gathered his things to leave, she found the courage to open up to him. "I'm sorry about the way things worked out between us."

"We're not done." He leaned over Hannah, kissed her forehead and whispered something in her ear.

"Anson, you're not hearing me. There is no 'us.'"

"Why, Tess? Why is that?"

"I've just never been…enough."

His expression went blank. "What on earth are you talking about?"

"Without my father and brother, I wasn't enough for my mother to fight to live. I wasn't enough for my husband to fight for our marriage." She held up a hand when it looked like he'd argue. "And I certainly wasn't enough for his parents. There will come a time that I won't be enough for you."

"Tess, honey, look at me." He knelt before her chair and cupped her face between his big hands. "You are more than enough. More than I ever hoped to find in a woman. You and Hannah have become my everything."

"You say that now, but—"

He captured her lips with a passionate, tender kiss. "I need you to hear what I'm saying. What I'm feeling. You might not need me, but I need you. I want to share a life with you and Hannah. Come back to me." He kissed her once more, then rose to his feet. At the door, he glanced over his shoulder, tension etching his face. "I love you, Tess."

Her heart jumped and fluttered, and she rushed to the doorway, but couldn't make herself go farther. She watched through a blur of tears as he strode down the long white corridor. He stopped once, and she thought he'd turn around. Instead, he continued forward until he crossed a patch of sunlight then disappeared into shadows.

The truth hit Tess like Thor's hammer, and she bit the inside of her cheek until the metallic tang of blood filled her mouth. She was completely in love with Anson Curry. And so was her daughter.

She was the only thing stopping them from being happy.

Chapter Seventeen

A few days later, arrangements were being made for Hannah's release. Relief that her daughter had made a quick and successful recovery was an understatement. Now that the surgery was done and the rest of their lives could begin, Tess finally let herself consider their future with clear eyes and a brighter outlook.

"We go home. See my Daddy and my Nan," Hannah told the doctor. "And my puppy."

"That's wonderful," he replied, and winked at her. "You can go home today after lunch. Mrs. Harper, don't hesitate to call if you have any questions or concerns."

She shook his hand. "Thank you so much for everything. Have a Merry Christmas."

"You, too. Bye, Hannah."

"Bye-bye, doctor man."

He chuckled on his way out the door.

Alone in the room once again, she watched Hannah chatter to Boo Bunny.

I could have lost her, but I didn't.

Tess hadn't allowed herself to chase after Anson, but she'd been thinking about his declarations. She picked up the photo he'd brought of the three of them on Thanksgiving and could no longer deny what she truly wanted. It was time to stop shutting love out and think about what she and Hannah needed. They had each other, but there was more than enough room in their hearts and lives for more people.

More family.

Even with the risks, a short time of magic was better than a lifetime of lonely days and nights. Better than a lifetime of regret for a chance passed up because of what *might* happen. Life was what you made of it in the time you had.

A burst of happiness pulled her cheeks into the biggest smile she'd felt in days. "Sweet girl, are you ready to go home to Oak Hollow?"

"I ready, Momma."

The evening was cold but sunny as they pulled up in front of Nan's big white Victorian house on Eighteenth Street. Before she could even get Hannah unbuckled from her seat, the front door opened, and Anson strode quickly down the walk. Still worried about the large incision on her daughter's chest, she carefully picked Hannah up and cradled her, then turned to face the man she loved.

"We home!" Hannah yelled.

Anson's eyes cut to her and she smiled. "We're home," she affirmed, and thought she saw a tear trickle down his cheek before he enveloped them both in a strong, but careful hug.

"For good?" he whispered against her ear.

"If it's not too late?"

"Never."

"Anson, I'm scared of doing something that might hurt my child, of having my heart broken. But most of all... I'm scared of living the rest of my life without you." Tess pulled back enough to see his face. "I love you."

He peppered each of them with kisses until they laughed. "I love you both. So much."

"Down, pease," Hannah requested. Once she was standing beside them on the sidewalk, she directed Anson and Tess to hold hands then took their free ones in hers. She held her arms wide and her eyes grew as big as saucers. "Circle! Momma, this my circle."

"Is it the one you've been looking for?" Anson asked.

The little girl giggled and squeezed their fingers harder. "Yes. My circle."

Tess's heart filled to bursting, and she met his loving gaze.

"A family circle," they said in unison.

On Christmas Eve, Anson led Tess and Hannah over to stand in front of the Christmas tree and dropped to one knee before them.

Tess's pulse raced and her cheeks ached from smiling, especially when he faced Hannah and opened a small jewelry box.

He pulled out a silver charm bracelet. A star, surrounded by a circle of colored gemstones, dangled from the center of the chain. "Will you be my daughter and take my last name?"

Tess gasped as a burst of tingling warmth shimmered through her chest, instantly making her world feel brighter.

"My Daddy!" Hannah squealed, and clapped her hands against his cheeks.

"My little one."

They hugged, and her daughter sat on her daddy's knee.

He clasped Tess's hand, pressed his lips to her knuckles and didn't try to hide his tears. "You are more than enough. You're the love I've been waiting for. Will you be my wife? Will the two of you be my family?"

"Yes, Anson. For as long as there are stars in the sky."

He slipped Nan's vintage, star-shaped ring onto

her finger, and when she knelt to join them, he kissed
her with the strength and gentleness of a man ready
to become a family of three.

* * * * *

Don't miss Makenna Lee's next book,
available June 2021 from
Harlequin Special Edition!

And in the meantime, check out these other
great single parent romances:

Home for the Baby's Sake
by Christine Rimmer

The Long-Awaited Christmas Wish
by Melissa Senate

In Service of Love
by Laurel Greer

SPECIAL EXCERPT FROM

⊕ HARLEQUIN
SPECIAL EDITION

*Brynn Hale, single mom widowed after an unhappy
marriage, has finally returned home to Starlight.
She's ready for a fresh start for her son, and what
better time for it than Christmas? But Nick Dunlap is
the one connection to her past she can't let go of...*

*Read on for a sneak peek at the next book in the
Welcome to Starlight miniseries,*
His Last-Chance Christmas Family
by Michelle Major.

"You sound like a counselor." The barest glimmer of
a smile played around the edges of Brynn's mouth.
"When did you get so smart, Chief Dunlap?"

"I was born this way. You never noticed before now
because you were too dazzled by my good looks."

Her eyes went wide for a moment, and he wondered
if he'd overstepped with the teasing. "I was dazzled
by you. That part is true." She rolled her eyes. "But I
guarantee you didn't show this kind of insight when we
were younger."

He should make some funny comment back to her,
keep the moment light. Instead, he let his gaze lower to
her mouth as he took the soft ends of her hair between

his fingers. "I might not have messed things up so badly if I had."

She drew in a sharp breath and he stepped away. This was not the time to spook her. "Come on, Brynn," he coaxed. "We both know it's not going to be good for anyone if you stay with your mom."

"She doesn't even want to meet Remi," Brynn told him, her full lips pressing into a thin line.

"Her loss," he said quietly. "All along it's been her loss. Say yes. Please."

She shifted and looked to where Tyler had disappeared with Kel. Without turning back to Nick, she nodded. "Yes," she said finally. "Thank you for the offer. I appreciate it and promise we won't disrupt your life." Now she did turn to him. "Very much, anyway," she added with a smile.

"Easy as pie," he said, ignoring the fact that his heart was beating as fast as if he'd just finished running a marathon.

Don't miss
His Last-Chance Christmas Family *by Michelle Major,*
available December 2020 wherever
Harlequin Special Edition books and ebooks are sold.

Harlequin.com

Love Harlequin romance?

DISCOVER.

Be the first to find out about promotions, news and exclusive content!

 Facebook.com/HarlequinBooks

Twitter.com/HarlequinBooks

Instagram.com/HarlequinBooks

Pinterest.com/HarlequinBooks

ReaderService.com

EXPLORE.

Sign up for the Harlequin e-newsletter and download a free book from any series at **TryHarlequin.com**

CONNECT.

Join our Harlequin community to share your thoughts and connect with other romance readers!
Facebook.com/groups/HarlequinConnection

HSOCIAL2020